I hope you guys enjoy the adventure!

STUCK

IT'S ABOUT TO GET VERY WEIRD ...

TIM BREWSTER

WCopyright © 2016 Tim Brewster.

Cover and interior images by Kaitlin Matthews

All rights reserved. No part of this book may be reproduced, stored, or transmitted by any means—whether auditory, graphic, mechanical, or electronic—without written permission of both publisher and author, except in the case of brief excerpts used in critical articles and reviews. Unauthorized reproduction of any part of this work is illegal and is punishable by law.

ISBN: 978-1-4834-5746-8 (sc)
ISBN: 978-1-4834-5745-1 (e)

Library of Congress Control Number: 2016913854

Because of the dynamic nature of the Internet, any web addresses or links contained in this book may have changed since publication and may no longer be valid. The views expressed in this work are solely those of the author and do not necessarily reflect the views of the publisher, and the publisher hereby disclaims any responsibility for them.

Any people depicted in stock imagery provided by Thinkstock are models, and such images are being used for illustrative purposes only. Certain stock imagery © Thinkstock.

Lulu Publishing Services rev. date: 09/22/2016

Contents

Chapter 1: It's about to Get Very Weird 1
Chapter 2: Weird Science 7
Chapter 3: 214 Years 14
Chapter 4: Weed Eaters 19
Chapter 5: Meat Eaters and Bug Crunchers 24
Chapter 6: The Machine 33
Chapter 7: Sierra has landed 40
Chapter 8: Get me out of here 44
Chapter 9: Okay, seriously? 51
Chapter 10: Wasteland 63
Chapter 11: Gymnastics for ~~Girls~~ Boy 69
Chapter 12: The Wall 80
Chapter 13: Wanigas 92
Chapter 14: Showdown 102
Chapter 15: Dimension Earth 112
Chapter 16: New Machine 117
About the Author 121

Chapter 1

It's about to Get Very Weird

I'm sitting at my desk, my fifth-grade desk, and I'm completely confused.

This doesn't make any sense! I'm thinking that I might be dreaming, so I pinch myself five times, but it doesn't work.

How could this *be*? This is my school. This is my classroom. This is my desk. This is where I always go on Mondays. The hall is the hall that I walked the same way as always. But something very weird is going on.

For starters, I don't recognize *anybody*. Not one single kid. Not one single teacher. Not even the front-desk lady. It's like every person I know in school has been scooped up and replaced by imposters.

They all *sort of* look like my friends, but not quite. The art on the walls is all there, and it's *sort of* as I remember it, but not quite. The classroom is *sort of* like my classroom. It has a strange look about it, like somebody who isn't a very good artist has just painted a picture of my life for me to live in. Even weirder is that everyone is treating me like they know me, just like my regular friends.

They keep saying things like, "Hey there! How was your weekend?" I give the best answer I can think of: "Uh, fine, I guess …"

Then a girl walks up and says, "Oh, wow, Tiarra! I love your new hair!"

"Tiarra?" I blurt out, confused.

"Ha ha ha," she says with a chuckle. "Yes, you. Like, don't you remember your own name?" the girl says as she walks away. My name is Sierra, not Tiarra!

I don't remember changing my hair or anything else, for that matter. I'm the same as yesterday; at least I think I am. I always leave my hair just hanging down to my shoulders. Or maybe a simple ponytail. My hair is blonde, wavy, and just fine the way it is when I wake up in the morning. Sometimes my dad insists that I at least do something with it, so I'll part it to one side and flip it up at the ends with the curling iron, but most of the time I just leave it. Seriously, it would have been a big day if I *had* changed my hair. I would rather spend my time building stuff and climbing trees in my jeans than fixing my hair. I like to wear my favorite purple hoodie over a T-shirt, and I don't care if my jeans and hoodie are worn out or dirty; they feel just fine to me. I love swinging from the monkey bars, so I'm strong, and I'm not scared of much, but today I'm definitely freaked out.

I think for a moment that it must be a mistake. Then the teacher I don't even recognize says "Tiarra, don't forget to hand in your homework." I see the whiteboard behind her. I read, "Mrs. LaPierre."

I'm confused. Our teacher didn't give homework on Friday. I just stare blankly at her. Mrs. LaPierre laughs. "Don't be a goof. I know you probably did next week's, too, Tiarra! Don't be shy." Then she points at my bag and smiles.

I undo the zipper on my bag and reach in with my hand. I'm kind of freaked out, like there might be a snake in there or something. My hand touches paper, and I look in. There it is—a book report. I pull it out and read the title. "The Stone Wizard, book report by Tiarra McMillan." I don't recognize it at all. That isn't even my last name! My name is Sierra Malkens, not Tiarra McMillan. *It's close to my name, but not quite ...*

"Okay, everyone, take your seats," Mrs. LaPierre says. "I'll be right back with our maps, so have a look at the words on the board." I look around at all the strangers, all getting settled in. I don't remember even *one* of their faces. It's so weird how I don't recognize them, but they recognize me as Tiarra. To me, everything is odd, but for them, I'm the only thing that seems a little different. I just don't get it. I remember the girl who said my hair was different. Maybe that's why they don't realize that I'm not Tiarra. They must think that I'm just Tiarra with a new hairstyle.

Then I see him. He's thin and a bit taller than me, and his short brown hair is sticking out in all directions, like he just got out of bed. His dark-brown eyes look like they are calculating something. He actually kind of looks like a young mad scientist, which would normally be cool because I love science, but right now I'd rather it be someone I recognize. He's wearing a T-shirt and jeans, like any boy, but they look like he's been wearing them for days.

I feel like I know him from *somewhere*, just *not here*.

He looks really nervous, and his eyes seem to dart around like he's a hungry alley cat. I recall those news stories about mad scientists who blow up their labs. *This is what they must look like just before they do it*, I think.

He's staring straight at me. His gaze is odd, like he is looking straight through me—about two hundred miles through me.

Then he gets up and starts walking toward me. He has a very serious look on his face, like he's coming over to pick a fight or something. As he gets closer, my hands make fists by themselves. The boy takes a quick glance around the room, and he's coming toward me even faster—I don't know what to do. My mind races, and for some reason, I suddenly wish that I had a stick or a rock or something—even my BB gun—just in case. I've been shooting BB guns for years. We never hunt or anything; we just shoot targets. My sister and I started shooting in competition about a year ago, and my dad says I'm a natural. I don't know if that's true, but I know that I can hit just about anything, and right now I wish I had my BB gun. I realize I'm overreacting, and I try to take a breath to calm down.

The boy walks right past me and slips a note onto my desk. Then he hurries back to his desk and sits down, staring hard at me again. He nods toward the note.

I look at the folded piece of paper and then back to the boy. He nods again. I open it slowly and read. The message makes my legs wobble and my hands shake. This is impossible. This can't be real. But I have no idea how very weird it's about to get.

The note

Chapter 2

Weird Science

I read the note again. And again.

It says, "Don't make trouble, or they will take you away. We have to get back to our dimension."

Take me away? Who? Where? What in the world is a *dimension*? I heard the word in the movie *Zoom*, where the bad brother had been locked away in another dimension. I think it might mean something about a different time and place. But other than that, I have no idea what this all means, and it's scaring me. I want to go home.

I'm jolted out of my thoughts by Mrs. LaPierre.

"All right, everyone. Let's look at the map of the world and where we are in the universe."

I love science. Space and astronomy are my favorite topics in science. At least this is my thing. It might help me to relax a bit.

Mrs. LaPierre pulls out a Frisbee-shaped piece of cardboard and holds it up, flat, like she's holding a plate of food. It has a map of the world on top. Mrs. LaPierre asks the class, "Who can tell me where we are?" A girl puts her hand up and Mrs. LaPierre calls out, "Yes, Julie?"

"We're on top!" answers Julie.

"That's right," Mrs. LaPierre says, pointing at a spot on top of the Frisbee map.

"Luckily, we're not close to the edge, because as you all know, people near the edge fall off the world sometimes!"

"People near the edge fall off sometimes," everyone in the class repeats.

Except for me.

This is bogus! The world isn't flat! It's a globe! It's a sphere, like a ball!

Mrs. LaPierre continues. "And can anyone tell me why it is light in the daytime and dark at night?"

A boy blurts out, "Because the sun flies around the flat earth, and when it goes *under* the earth, it's nighttime."

"Correct!" Mrs. LaPierre says, pointing her finger at the boy and smiling. "These are the fundamentals!"

I'm shaking. I'm going to lose it. Fundamentals! Fundamental. *Mental* is right! Everyone knows that the earth revolves around the sun.

I half raise my hand to say something. Mrs. LaPierre says, "Yes, Tiarra?"

"Uh, well, I think ..." But just then I look at the boy, who is shaking his head at me. I remember his warning.

Don't make trouble, or they will take you away.

"Tiarra, spit it out," Mrs. LaPierre says.

"Oh, I think, uh ... that it sure must be scary to live near the edge of the world."

"Oh yes, I imagine it is," Mrs. LaPierre says. "Okay, everyone, read the chapter in your science workbook on how our earth formed and how we know it's flat."

I try to read, but I just can't. It's all so crazy—and just plain wrong. I flip pages all morning until the recess bell rings.

I get on my coat and runners and head outside. A girl comes up to me and asks whether I want to play on the monkey bars. I say I'd rather not—I'm not feeling well. I sit down on a rock, and I feel like screaming.

Just then the nervous-looking boy comes over and sits down beside me.

"It's okay," he says. "I know how you feel. I went through the same thing ... my name is Tom."

I grit my teeth. "What is going on? Who are these people? Where am I? I want to go home!"

"You can't go home yet. Your real parents aren't there."

"What? My real parents? What are you talking about?"

"They're in another dimension," Tom says as he pushes sand with his shoes.

"What? What does that mean? What dimension?" I demand.

"Well, it's hard to explain," Tom says.

"Why don't you *try*!" I shout.

"Okay, okay, easy, don't make a scene," Tom says, looking around to see whether anyone heard me.

"Okay. Imagine that somewhere, way out in space, in another time, maybe millions of years before, or even millions of years after, our time, there is a world. It's identical to ours, like looking in the mirror."

"Okay," I say.

"So there's this mirror world, and it's identical to ours. It's like a copy. Same people, same trees, same everything. There's even a copy of you in this other world. There's a copy of your family, a copy of your yard, a copy of your house. That's called another dimension. It's a different place and time where there is another version of this world."

"But they aren't identical," I say. "Everything here is a bit off."

"Yeah," Tom says, "Every version is different, and this one must be pretty close to yours."

"But what does that have to do with me and this place?"

"Well, somehow, the two identical worlds, these two dimensions got connected by a wormhole."

I interrupt again.

"A *what*? Did you just say worm hole?"

"Yes," says Tom. "Just concentrate here, I know it's weird."

"Oh, d'ya think?" I say sarcastically.

Tom continues. "A wormhole has nothing to do with worms. It's just called that. It's more like some kind of time tunnel through space. We got sucked through it, and our copies went to our real world."

"You mean I traveled through space?" I blurt out.

"And time," Tom sighs. "We're stuck in this other dimension, this other copy of our world. Meanwhile, the copies of you and me, our twins, are stuck in *our* dimension, back home. Basically, we switched places with our twins from the other dimension. We're stuck."

"What the heck do you mean, stuck?" I ask.

"We're stuck here."

My head was swimming. I feel sick. Why me?

"Are we stuck here forever? I want to go home! My *real* home. To my dad and my sister!"

I start to sob. The reality hits me the moment I say it out loud. My dad, and my sister, Samantha. Sam is only eight, and she must be terrified that I'm missing. We fight a lot, like most sisters, but we're very close, and I feel a big hole without Sam here, just like I felt when mom went away. My dad had to suffer through that, but he always used to say that he was so grateful that he still had me and Sam. Now I'm gone.

I keep thinking, *What would mom do right now?* It's what I always do when I'm scared or unsure of something. Mom was so smart; she was a scientist. She studied high-energy particles at a lab in the city. She was always so excited about her work. And then one day two years ago she went missing. The police and my dad tried everything but couldn't find any clues, other than that she arrived at work one day but didn't leave. She was never seen again, and it just about destroyed my dad ... and me. Sam was too young to understand, but it was hard on all of us.

I'm not sure I can handle this. So I grit my teeth and close my eyes and think, *What would mom do right now?* I know what mom would do. She'd figure it out. She'd stop and make a mental list of all the information she had and all the tools she could use. That's what she would do. Dad would say, "Suck it up, and do something!" I realize I need to listen to both. I have to suck it up *and* figure it out.

"I need to figure this out and get home," I say to Tom.

"I know," Tom says, putting his hand on my shoulder. "Me, too, and I think I know how."

I start to feel a bit better. I'm starting to think maybe I can trust Tom. I don't feel so alone now.

"Okay," I say, feeling more confident now. "What do we have to do?"

"Well," Tom starts, "I have a plan, and I think it will work. I hope it will work, because I've been trapped here way too long."

"How long, exactly?" I ask slowly. "How long have you been ... stuck?"

Tom looks at me nervously and then glances away. Then he looks me right in the eyes and says with a very tired voice, "Two hundred and fourteen years."

Our flat Earth

Chapter 3

214 Years

Two hundred and fourteen years.

I am in shock. Just when I thought it was getting better, it got worse. *Way* worse. Just when I thought I found someone to help me, I find out that he's in deeper trouble than I am.

Two hundred and fourteen years deeper.

For the rest of the day, I don't hear anything anyone says. It's all just a blur. My mind races. But I become more and more set in my mind that I am going to figure this out. I'm not going to be stuck here for two hundred and fourteen years. Tom is my best—no, my *only*—chance as far as I can see, so we're partners, teammates. If Tom has a plan, then I'm going to help him.

At the end of the day, as I'm getting ready to leave, the principal comes over to me. I can see his school name tag:

"Principal Wanigas." It's a strange name, and it suits him, because he looks strange to me. Principal Wanigas is tall and sort of thin, with a slight hunch in his shoulders. His tan hair is thin on top, and he has a big, pointy nose and beady eyes. He sort of looks like a vulture. I'm creeped out the moment he looks at me, the way a mouse might feel when it notices that it's being watched by a snake.

"Tiarra, your teacher says you've been acting strange today. Even in science, your favorite subject. Are you okay?"

I look at him, and I feel nervous. He has a strange look on his face. He doesn't look like he's concerned about me—more like he is ... suspicious. I wonder if he's the "they" that the note was talking about. Maybe Principal Wanigas will take me away. Or maybe my imagination is out of control. Either way, I'm not taking any chances.

"No, uh, I'm fine," I reply. "I just have a bit of a tummy ache is all."

"Well, I hope you get better," Principal Wanigas says.

"Thanks," I say and walk out the doors into the schoolyard.

Tom is waiting for me there. "I know you're upset, but I—"

"Don't worry about it," I interrupt. "I want to hear your plan. I am *not* going to be here for two hundred and fourteen years, and I want to start fixing this right now."

"Good," Tom says. "Let's go."

"Where are we going?"

"To my place. I can explain the whole thing."

"Start explaining now," I order. "I don't want to wait. I need to know everything. Like how you can be here for two hundred and fourteen years and still be a kid in grade five. Why aren't you old? You should be like, all old and wrinkly, and sort of ... dead."

"Yeah, I know. Listen. Here's the thing. I have a time machine, and ..."

I laugh out loud.

"Hey, I'm serious!" Tom protests.

"I know, and I believe you. Why wouldn't I? After all, I'm stuck in this place, too. I just realized that you said 'time machine' and I totally believed you."

As we talk, I wander toward a crosswalk. "No!" Tom shouts. "Get away from the crosswalk! It's not safe."

I back up, and Tom pulls me over to the grass, away from where I was standing.

"C'mon, we'll take the path over here."

"But why did you —"

"Look," Tom says. "In about ten seconds a car is going to crash in that crosswalk."

I look at him, confused. "But how can you ..."

Just then I hear the tires squealing behind me. I turn and watch as a black car speeds up, going way too fast for the corner before the crosswalk. It starts to slide, hits the curb and slams into a tree just inches from where I had been standing a few moments ago. I'm trembling.

"Hits it every time!" Tom laughs as he turns and walks up the path between the houses.

"How did you know?" I ask. "How in the world did you know?"

"Okay," Tom says, "Every time I use the time machine, I get partway through the wormhole home, and I get pulled back, and I end up back here, back in the same time and place where I started. I keep living the same thing over and over."

"You get pulled back? How does that work? I don't get it."

"I'm not totally sure myself," Tom admits. "It's like my twin just fights it somehow, and I get sent back. It's almost like both twins have to really want to switch back—like he, or something else, really doesn't want me to get back."

"So you just live this day over and over?"

"Yep. Or sometimes I've just stayed for years, but no matter what, when I try the machine, I end up back at Day One again."

I stop walking. I begin to have a thought that scares me. I feel the hair on the back of my neck stand up.

I ask Tom, very slowly, "Tom, why would your twin not want you to leave?"

Tom stops in his tracks.

"I don't know. But wait till you meet his parents ..."

Chapter 4

Weed Eaters

I'm stopped dead in my tracks by what I see.

Tom and I pull open the gate to his backyard. The entire yard is a massive, colorful jungle of weeds as high as the house. I can't even see the house. It's like a huge, green, leafy, monster house. The path leading to the house is just a dark, narrow, green tunnel, with huge plants and flowers hunched over the walkway like monsters. It creeps me out, and I don't waste time following directly behind Tom.

Tom looks up at the weedy walls and grins. "Hungry?" he asks, opening the door to the house.

We step in the back door and start down the hall to his room, and Tom calls out, "Hi, Mom! I'm home."

A woman's voice comes from the other side of the house. "Oh hi, honey!" It's a cheery and friendly-sounding voice, so that's a good sign. Then the voice says, "Don't be too long, we have a wonderful dandelion salad for supper tonight! And your favorite—stinkweed stew!"

My jaw drops. "Did she just say stinkweed stew?" I whisper.

"Yup."

"And that's your favorite?"

"No," Tom replies. "I hate it. But it's easier to go along with it. They're complete fruitcakes. It's like living with Willy Wonka, except it's weeds instead of chocolate."

I look at Tom like he's kidding me, but I can see from his expression that he's serious. We go down the hall on the right to a room, and I catch glimpses of family photos on the wall. Tom and his parents at the park or at a lake, and everyone is always smiling. It is the first time I feel some hope, some relief, that there are good people in this dimension. Tom opens the door at the end of the room, and I read the sign: "Enter at Own Risk."

"Is it safe in there?" I ask.

"Yeah, this is my room."

Tom sees me looking at the sign and says, "I put the sign there so they still think I'm a normal kid."

I had almost forgotten that Tom has been here a long time, trying to get by, trying to get home, trying not to get found out. I can't help but wonder exactly what it is he has to hide from, and who will "take him away."

Just then his mother—the mother, I mean—calls out from the kitchen, "Supper's ready!"

"C'mon," Tom says, "let's go eat, and I'll take you to the lab after supper."

We walk back down the hall and around the corner to the kitchen, and I'm floored at what I see. The whole table is filled with pots and platters filled with every kind of plantlike dish I could imagine. I don't recognize anything, but it looks and smells wonderful. The room is thick with the aroma of roses, berries, corn, beans, and sweet sauces. Then it hits me: I am *starving*! I wait for Tom, and he signals for me to sit down beside him at the near end of the table. Tom's mom turns around, and I am immediately at ease: she looks like anybody's mom. She has long, curly brown hair and soft eyes. She is wearing a flowery apron that says, "More peas!" and she is humming as she brings a steaming bowl of dandelions to the table.

"So, Tom, are you going to introduce us to your guest?" she asks as Tom's dad strolls into the kitchen. He's holding the newspaper and pushing his glasses up on his nose. He also looks friendly, and he smiles as he sits down. He is wearing a plain sweater over a shirt and tie. He could be a math teacher from the old days, with his short-cropped black hair and neat outfit.

"Oh yeah, this is a friend from school. She really likes science, too, so she's going to help me with my projects," Tom says as he scoops some green, slimy broth into both our bowls.

"Do you like stinkweed stew?" his mom asks.

"Oh, uh, sure, yep," I answer. "I mean, it doesn't beat a good steak, but your stew smells great!"

21

I wait for the friendly laugh I expect, but it doesn't come.

I see that Tom's mom and dad are frozen, and they are staring at me like I just popped a bird out of my ear. Tom's dad looks at me sternly and asks in a cold, level voice, "You aren't one of *those,* are you?"

Tom's mom is looking nervously from me to Tom and back to the dad. I'm petrified. What did I say? What did he mean by "one of those?"

Suddenly, the warm, fuzzy family atmosphere had just gotten really, really cold.

Tom's Parents

Chapter 5

Meat Eaters and Bug Crunchers

"In this house we won't tolerate …" the dad starts again.

Tom interrupts with a laugh and gives me a nervous glance. "Ha ha, no, Dad. It's slang for beets. Beet steak we call it at school, for the big ones, you know, the really big ones. Seriously, you guys are such nerds!"

"Oh, uh, okay, then, Tom," his dad says. "You gave me a scare there. You kids with your crazy new words."

I have no idea what Tom is talking about, but it was a nice save; he clearly made that up on the spot. Tom's mom regains her happy demeanor and returns to serving the dinner.

"You sure fooled me," she laughs. "At least you're not one of those awful bug-crunchers!"

"Sierra, a bug cruncher? As if!" Tom snaps.

Tom's mom and dad have frozen again, and they exchange a serious glance. "Did you say her name was Sierra?" Tom's mom asks carefully.

"Uh, I mean, Tiarra," Tom answers, and he is fidgeting nervously.

"Oh, well, Sierra, Tiarra, either way, we've been waiting for you for a long time," Tom's mom says as she sets more food on the table. I notice that Tom's dad give her a long concerned glance.

"Huh? For me?" I ask, and I'm starting to feel a bit worried. I glance at Tom, and he shrugs.

Tom's dad jumps in, "Well, uh, you know, for Tom to have an actual friend— any friend—for once, that's all."

Waiting for me? Bug crunchers? What in the world? This just gets weirder every minute. If someone had made this story up, I'd have told them that they were a mental case.

Tom nudges me with his elbow and nods at the stew. I dip my spoon in carefully. I look up and see Tom's mom and dad both looking at me, like they want to know for sure. I know I have to prove myself here, so I dig my spoon in right to the bottom and scoop up a heaping mound of green slime. It looks like someone took eggs, seaweed, grass, and rotten bananas, put them in a blender, and turned it into a mushy, slimy mulch. I feel myself almost gag, but I know I have to hold it together. I shove the whole thing in my mouth. I think I'm going to barf, but then the taste hits.

It's good. It's *really* good.

I gulp it down, and my hunger takes over.

I think to myself, *Well, I haven't eaten since I crossed the universe ... of course I'm hungry!* I shovel in scoop after scoop until the bowl is empty.

When I finally stop, I look up and all three of them are staring at me with their jaws hanging open. Even Tom looks shocked.

I know I have to break the ice.

"Wow! I can see why this stew is your favorite, Tom!" I exclaim. Everyone breaks out in laughter, and I know I'm good to go. Tom's mom and dad visibly relax and start an easygoing conversation about work, asking us about school, and passing trays of delicious, weedy food around. It all tastes wonderful, and I feel relaxed and safer than I have felt all day.

When Tom's mom and dad get up from the table to clear the dishes, Tom smiles and winks at me and whispers, "Nice work."

I smile back, thinking that I don't know why he hates the food, because it was really delicious. I wasn't pretending. I decide not to tell him I liked it, because I think it helps him trust me if he thinks I was pretending. Either way, everyone's happy, and I'm full.

Tom and I get up from the table and help clean up. It's clear that this is a happy family, and it makes me miss my family even more. When I get back, I'm going to make stinkweed stew for them. I almost laugh out loud as I think about putting that one in for the school recipe book. They'll think I've lost my mind, and then when they see it, they'll lock me up for sure. I realize they'll never try it, because they won't be across the table from weed-eating crazies from the mental dimension. But I know Sam will try it. All I'll have to do is dare her. She can't pass up a dare, *ever*. Last camping trip she ate a giant worm on a dare. I smile just thinking about it.

Sam. I have to get back to Sam, even just to see her eat the weed-slime.

Finally Tom heads for the back door. "See ya, we're going to the lab."

"Okay, Tom, be careful with all that stuff," his mom says. "I still wish we knew what you were making."

"Oh, just a time machine to another dimension," Tom says over his shoulder.

"As if!" the dad says, and everyone starts laughing. Then his dad's tone turns more serious. "Listen, just be careful in there! We don't want Tiarra to get hurt with your invention, or her mom won't be happy. Do you understand?"

"Ya, Dad, got it."

We head out the door and down the dark garden path. I look back, and both Tom's parents are standing at the window watching us leave. I see them turn and hug each other. They're still hugging when we get out of sight. They seem awfully happy that Tom has a friend ... or maybe it's just me ...

As we walk, turning right at the end of his yard, it's getting even darker because the sun is setting, but somehow not as menacing as before. The sky is red and yellow and orange as we head toward the forest at the end of Tom's street. I can hear the laughter and shouts of small children and the hum of lawnmowers. We reach the end of the street with the big, dark forest in front of us. Tom turns and walks alongside it for a ways and then stops and looks back to see whether anyone is looking. He waves me closer and says, "Now," and darts into the bushes. I follow, and we head down a dirt path that winds downhill, deeper into the forest.

As we hike along, I notice all the weeds. I decide that now I like weeds, although they still don't beat a good steak. It reminds me of the "one of those" comment.

"What did they mean by 'one of those'?" I ask as we wind down the path.

"Here's the thing," Tom starts, "There are three types of people in this world. The Weed Eaters, the Meat Eaters, and the Bug Crunchers. None of them likes the others ... at all."

"But we have vegetarians and stuff back home," I say.

"No, it's different," Tom says. It's more than just food choice here. They can't stand each other. Their whole lifestyle is different. The Weed Eaters are normal, nice. Most of the world are Weed Eaters. And everyone thinks eating meat turns you crazy. The Meat Eaters *are* crazy ... like really nutty hippies, but harmless. Meat obviously doesn't make you crazy, but since the only ones here willing to try meat are the nutcases ... the myth goes on."

"But what about scientists? Don't they see it isn't true? Don't they tell people it isn't true?" I ask.

"Remember back home, how everyone always goes on fad diets all the time, even though it has been proven that crash dieting doesn't work? It's like that, but more extreme. Everyone just really believes this stuff."

"That's insane," I say.

"Oh, yeah, you should see the game show here called 'Hold It Down,'" Tom says. "People go on this show and eat stuff, and if they don't barf, they win. For us, it would be awesome, because it's always like, hot dogs or roast or whatever, but they think it's so gross. They always bring out bacon last, and it gets 'em every time. Total bacon barf-o-rama!"

I shout back, "I could go on that show right now! Bacon! They could pay *me* to eat bacon!"

Man, I think, a whole society, a whole world that believes these myths. It can't be that simple.

"What about the Bug Crunchers?"

Tom ducks under a low-hanging branch and holds it up for me. "That's the really freaky part." The Weed Eaters and Meat Eaters can't stand each other, but they both hate the Bug Crunchers. And the Bug Crunchers hate everything, even each other. Seriously, they're mean. The kids in school that always fight with everyone? Bug Crunchers. The teacher that is always yelling ? Total Bug Cruncher."

"Okay, wait," I stop him. "They eat bugs ... like for real?"

"Yep. But not just bugs. All the grossest poisonous ones. The ones with venom, like scorpions and spiders."

"Ugh," I say. "Why would anyone do that?"

"That's the weird thing," Tom says. "It's like they get addicted to it. And honestly, something about it all smells funny."

"Duh, like bugs smell funny!" I laugh, but Tom remains serious.

"No," he continues. "I mean it always seems like certain people are Bug Crunchers. The ones who enforce things. The ones who keep people in line. But that's not the weirdest part."

Based on what I've seen in this world so far, I know there's always more.

"The thing is," he says, "that I've been here a long time, like more than five generations, and the jumps are getting more consistent."

"What do you mean?" I ask.

"Like where I land, how it feels. It's like a path gets worn by hikers. It feels like my jumps are wearing a path."

"Another thing," I say, "Why was your dad so concerned about me? And that comment about waiting for me?" I ask.

"I have no idea," Tom says. "But they've never showed any interest in what I do until you came along. They've never been so excited about a guest for dinner, and that was the biggest meal we've ever had. They brought out all the good stuff, like they were expecting a special guest or something."

I feel a chill down my spine. Maybe they really were expecting me. What makes me so special, and how would they know? But they seemed genuinely nice, and I can't help but feel that they are good people—that they must be good people.

Just then we reach a huge car-size stump. Tom grabs a knot in the wood and twists it. There is clear "clinking" sound, and a hatch opens to a dark tunnel just big enough to walk in, hunched over.

"Whoa, is this where the time-machine is?"

"Yep."

"I can't believe you're really going into a time machine," I say.

Tom stops climbing in the hatch and looks back at me.

"I'm not. You are."

Chapter 6

The Machine

I follow Tom down the dark tunnel.

The walls and roof are narrow and low, so I have to crouch down and walk hunched over. I try to look past Tom to see where we're going, but his body blocks almost the whole tunnel ahead. It feels cold and damp, the floor and walls seem to be made of clay, and it slopes downward. It's dark, but there is a very slight light coming from a crack up ahead, and my eyes start to adjust.

Tom reaches the spot where the strip of light is peeking through and grabs a handle hidden in a root on the wall. A wooden door creaks open to reveal a large, warm, well-lit room. We step inside, and I can stand up fully now.

"Welcome to the lab," Tom says, gesturing for me to come in with a half bow.

I'm speechless. It's like we just stepped into Batman's secret hideout. It's about the size of a one-car garage, but shaped like a stone cave, with round, bumpy walls and a dome-shaped roof. All around the room there are light bulbs hanging from hooks pounded into the hard clay walls. At the far end, there is a little electric heater, and it is blowing a warm breeze across the room. There are electrical wires and extension cords everywhere connected to everything. There is a little wooden table and chairs on my right, and a lantern and some books sit atop the table. On my left is a big whiteboard on a wooden stand, with papers taped all over it and math equations, diagrams, and notes everywhere.

But the part that really grabs my attention is the giant, round arch in the middle of the room. It looks like a big, shiny yellow hula hoop standing up, except that the hoop is as thick as a rain spout, and big enough around to walk through. The hoop is wrapped in thin golden wire so that you can't even see what the hoop is made of underneath. Attached to the hoop at the bottom is a giant, thick cable that runs to a hole in the wall at the back of the room. A computer is sitting on a small desk by the hoop, and it is connected to the hoop with more wires.

The wire sparkles, and I put my hand out slowly to touch it. Then I look at Tom. He nods. I put my finger on it, and I feel it start to vibrate a little, exactly to the beat of my heart, and I snap my hand back in fear.

"Potentium," Tom says. "It won't hurt you. It's Latin for power metal—a new element. It absorbs power or energy and then magnifies it and sends it out as a perfectly matched and much stronger version of that energy. It's the most powerful transmitter of energy known."

Tom is speaking like an old scientist, like an old man who has been studying at a university for years, not like a kid in grade five. For a second it seems odd, and I almost have to remind myself that Tom has been here for over two hundred years.

"Where did you get the ... how did you build ... how do you know?" I stutter.

Tom points at the table, and we go sit down, and he gets a couple of juice boxes from a small fridge under the table. He tells me how he first built a small hideout just to try to escape the horrible situation he was in. How he started to learn things. How he decided to do something. He tells me how a couple of times he actually stayed here and got really old and got his hands on some potentium in a job he had and brought it back with him when he got bounced back here to the beginning.

"But why do you get brought back to the beginning, but your machine is still here?"

"I dunno," he says, staring at the large gold hoop. "It's like it affects living things, and the things you are wearing, or holding, but the other stuff you leave behind, it stays as you left it."

"So in a way, you are changing this dimension."

"I guess," he sighs. "But not enough to get home ... yet."

While we drink juice and sit at the table, I listen to Tom tell his story, and I realize for the first time just how hard this ordeal has been for him. I knew it was a long time, but to hear the story in detail, it seems longer.

Over two hundred years. More than three lifetimes.

A hundred years ago he found a way to get potentium back here and started building the machine. That's when he started trying to get home. He had been trying for almost fifty years when I came along.

"Tom, I'm so sorry," I say. I feel ashamed how I felt sorry for myself when I first got here, on my first day, compared to what Tom has been through.

"So how does it work?" I ask, trying to get the conversation back on a more positive note.

"Well," Tom starts, standing up and pointing at the large cable. "The power comes from the city power grid. Took me twenty-two years to dig it in. Almost died twice when the cable tunnel caved in on me. The power runs through the potentium and gets magnified, and by controlling the flow, I can control whether I go forward or back, or how far in time. But as I explained, it just doesn't stick. I always get bounced."

"But it's just power," I say. "How does that send you anywhere?"

"Somehow there is an exact amount of power needed to rip a hole in a dimension. Remember the movie *Back to the Future*? It's like that, except it takes a lot less than the 1.21 gigawatts of electricity from the movie, and it affects more than time."

"So is it safe?"

"I'm still here," Tom says.

I think about how I'm going to have to go into that thing. For real. I know I have to. It won't work for Tom, and I need to try.

What would Mom do? Figure it out, Sierra. What would Dad do? Suck it up, kid.

"Okay, so what's the plan? Where am I headed?" I ask. I'm terrified, but I try to sound brave. I squeeze my fists so Tom won't see my hands shaking.

Tom seems to perk up. Maybe he finally believes I'm in for the full game.

"We'll start with a test. Send you back, and we hope that you'll get there, and then I bring you back, and we learn something. Something that will help us solve this for good."

It never occurred to me that Tom might have to bring me back. Maybe that means I would have a choice. What if I get home and don't want to come back here? Would I abandon Tom? My mind is racing as Tom starts to click away at the keyboard, and the hoop starts to hum louder and louder.

"How do you bring me back?"

"Once you get there, don't stay too long, no more than an hour, and then go back to the exact spot you landed, and as long as you have this chunk of potentium in your hand, you should come back. At this end, I will reverse the energy flow, and back you come."

Tom places a small piece of potentium the size of a grape in my hand. I feel the energy humming through my whole body.

"Okay, stand back a minute … ten seconds …"

Suddenly there's a loud crack and a flash of greenish-gold light. I jump back and cover my eyes. I carefully open them and look where the hoop used to be. Now there's a big, shimmering green ball of light, and the whole thing is humming and buzzing so loud I have to cover my ears.

"It's ready!" Tom shouts.

He comes over and yells to me over the noise. "You've only got about thirty seconds before it becomes unstable. Listen, it's safe. You've got to trust me. Go back and check it out, and don't lose the potentium. And, please, please, come back."

I look directly into Tom's eyes, and I can see how hard this is for him. He's trusting me to come back for him, not to abandon him once I'm home.

I can't show him my fear, my doubt. I can hear my dad's voice in my head. *Suck it up Sierra. It's like taking off a Band-Aid ... just rip it, girl, just rip it.*

"See you in an hour," I say, and I step into the ball of light.

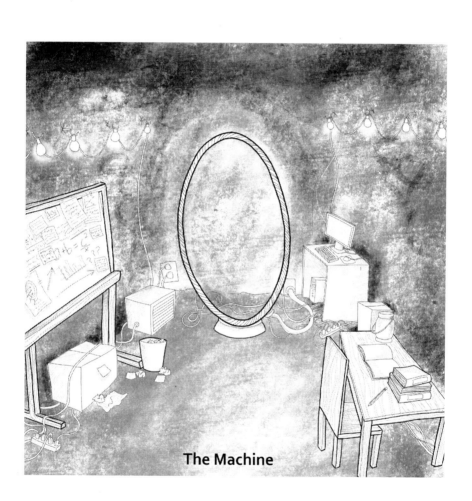
The Machine

Chapter 7

Sierra has landed

I'm on the wildest free-falling waterslide I've ever been on.

But it's not water. It's some kind of blinding lightning slide, and it's making me motion-sick. I feel like I'm in an invisible rocket ship, blasting through the universe. I'm sure I can see constellations I know, but some of them are backward ... like maybe I'm seeing them from the other side.

Then I see her.

It's me, but it's not quite me.

Tiarra.

She looks kind of blurry and out of focus. She also looks as scared as I feel. She is going the other way, and I think I can actually feel her. We are connected. I know it. I think as hard as I can in my head, *It's okay*, and I feel her relax a bit. Then she's gone.

Silence. A breeze. Children laughing. Everything feels right.

I'm home.

I'm standing on the sidewalk right where it started to get weird before, in *my* town, *my* dimension.

"It works, Tom," I whisper to myself.

I start to feel happy. Normal. Relieved. Excited.

I'm home! I don't ever want to leave here again, but I know I have to. Tom needs me. I have to do the right thing here.

Then I remember Sam! And Dad!

The realization that I will see them again hits me like I've won the lottery. I start sprinting home, full speed, jumping over bushes, across roads, over fences. My lungs and legs are burning, but I'm not slowing down. I see our house, and I can barely contain myself. Everything looks normal. I'm so out of breath I can barely speak, but I burst in the front door screaming their names.

And then I freeze. Something isn't right. It's really, creepily, quiet.

I listen carefully and I hear a muffled noise in Sam's bedroom.

I start walking to the room slowly. "Sam?" I say cautiously.

I hear footsteps scurrying in her room.

"Sam? It's me, Sierra."

Nothing.

TIM BREWSTER

I walk into the room and see that the closet is closed. I hear breathing behind the closet door. I get all of my courage up, grit my teeth, grab the handle, and open the closet.

What I see terrifies me. The fear rises in my stomach, and I grip the potentium hard in my hand. I'm paralyzed by confusion, and my brain is screaming for Tom to please take me back to that other dimension, to get me out of here, *now*.

Because *that* ... is *not* my sister.

Sierra - Tiarra Flyby

Chapter 8

Get me out of here

This nightmare just got worse.

This means that my sister is in big trouble. My mind races, and I want to run, but I can't.

She looks exactly like my sister, but not quite.

The little girl in the closet is sitting with her back against the wall of the closet under the hanging clothes, with her arms wrapped around her knees. She looks as scared as I feel, and I can see that she has been crying. It's obvious she has been in hiding for a while. On the floor around her there are crumpled bags of crackers, cereal bowls, and empty juice boxes. She has made a kind of fort in the closet with blankets and boxes. She stares back at me with her big green eyes, tears slipping down her cheeks, and she is waiting for me to say something.

She is Stuck.

This is my sister's twin. Like me and my sister, she must be confused, terrified, and lonely. I crouch down on one knee and reach out to her, but she flinches. I see that I'll have to calm her down. I have to tell her what Sam would want to hear. I pull my hands back and start again.

"My name is Sierra. I'm a friend of Tiarra's. I know this must be really weird and scary for you, but you can trust me."

She blinks and whispers, "Wh-where is Tiarra? Where's my mom?"

"I had the same questions. Listen, they are both okay. I am trying to sort out this problem, too."

"Who are you?" She asks. "Why do you look so much like Tiarra?"

I think about how to explain this in a way that she will understand—and believe. I decide that I'll tell her the way I would tell my sister. She's Sam's twin, so it's about as close as I could get.

Sam.

I don't have time to go through this whole thing. I have to get back. I realize I have no idea how long I've been here, or whether it's been too long. If I stay too long and Tom can't get me back, my sister will trapped forever. I think of her, scared and confused in hiding somewhere in that other world, completely alone in that dimension. I don't even have a way to tell Tom to look after her. It makes me sick just thinking about it. I would rather be trapped there than let my sister go through it. I have to help this girl and get moving fast.

"Listen, it's kind of hard to explain. What is your name?"

She looks at me like she is trying to decide whether to trust me, and then she says "Tabatha, but my sister calls me Tabby."

"Okay, Tabatha, I need you to trust me, to believe me. I'm in the same boat you are. I'm from far away, and somehow Tiarra and I got switched, and now so did you and my sister Sam."

Tabatha leans forward and her eyes brighten. "Tiarra disappeared today ... there was a bright light."

This must have been when I got here. It didn't occur to me that my twin would be yanked away from wherever she was when I jumped, using the machine.

"I know. I saw the same thing. I am going to try to get you and Tiarra home, and I need you to just carry on like everything is normal."

"My parents ..." Tabatha says.

"Just trust me, my dad is awesome. Just act as normal as possible."

Tabatha looks at me warily and nods slowly.

"How long is this going to take?"

"I don't know. I'm sorry. But just stick with Tiarra. She'll be back in a few minutes, and I think she might understand now."

I get up to leave and Tabatha leaps out and practically tackles me with a big hug around my neck. She squeezes so hard it almost chokes me, but I hug back. It feels like I'm hugging Sam, and I feel the connection. We're all connected.

Sam.

"Okay, I gotta go." I release her and stand up. She slowly gets up and out of the closet, and her eyes are looking scared again.

"Listen, where were you when Tiarra disappeared?" I ask her.

"Right here." says Tabatha.

"Okay, wait here, and she will be back, I promise. Tell her about me, and tell her I am working on it."

"Okay." Says Tabatha.

"Oh, one more thing. Tell Dad that you and Tiarra are doing an experiment at school, so you can't eat meat, okay?"

Tabatha looks at me questioningly and nods.

"Oh, and someday I will cook you the best stinkweed stew you ever ate."

Tabatha giggles and hugs me again, and I leave the house through the back door. I stop at the garage on the way out because I need something with me from now on, just in case. I grab my BB gun, quickly load it with BBs, and start running.

I'm clutching the little potentium ball in my free hand as I run down the street back to the spot where I landed, thinking about how this little ball of gold metal is my only way of getting back to my sister. I wish I had gotten more time, the chance to see my dad, too. I came all the way back here, and I didn't get to see either my dad or my sister. Now I have to go back there, to find Sam. I'm almost back to the spot, and I'm not even sure anymore which world I'm headed back to. I can't even keep it straight anymore, with all this zapping back and forth. Twin World. That's where I'm going.

I reach the spot and squeeze the potentium ... and wait.

Nothing happens for what seems like an hour. I see kids playing down the street. I recognize people walking their dogs. I wish it were all normal again, so I wouldn't have to go back.

Then the ball of light explodes in my eyes, and I'm streaking across time and space again. It's starting to make me feel sick. I wonder what would happen if I barfed ... would my barf arrive there, too? I wonder if my barf has a twin version as well. What if astronauts found my breakfast splattered all over the moon someday. I laugh out loud as I imagine NASA talking to the astronauts. "Say again mission commander ... did you say there's, um, human vomit there??"

Before I know it I'm lying on the ground in the grass field near Tom's house.

Twin World.

I try to shake the fuzziness out of my head as I get up, and my legs are still a bit shaky. It's not easy being a dimension jumper.

I need to get Sam, but Tom's house is closer, and I have no idea how long I've been gone anymore, so I decide to swing by there first because if he's there, he can help me get Sam. I run around the back to his gate and up the weed tunnel. I don't see or hear any movement inside. I knock, but there's no answer, and the door is hanging open a bit. Nobody is home, but the door is open.

That's odd.

I slip inside and tiptoe down the hall toward Tom's room. I don't even know why I'm tiptoeing.

Tom's door is open just a crack, and I read the sign "Enter at Own Risk." For some reason I get an uneasy feeling that it means something this time. I'm about to push Tom's door open when I get a glimpse through the opening.

Tom is sitting on the bed scratching his arm very slowly. Just when I'm about to say hello, his fingers dig into the skin on his arm, and he peels back a rubbery-looking flap, and I see the inside of his arm. It's not what a person's arm should look like. It's all electronic parts and gears and tiny blinking lights.

I gasp and cover my mouth with my hand to block the sound. I stand stone-still, and my heart almost stops for a second.

Then Tom glances up, and he doesn't look right. His eyes are red, with a silver, diamond-shaped spot in the center. I flinch and bump the door open, and his head snaps over to look right at me, and he blinks with one red eye—and it makes the sound of a camera taking a picture.

I turn and run for my life.

Robot Tom!

Chapter 9

Okay, seriously?

I crash through the back door and sprint down the path through the weed tunnel.

Just as I get to the back gate, I turn and look back. Maybe I just imagined it. Maybe I'm losing my mind. Maybe I should take my gun and give him one, just for being a robot ...

Before I can do anything, robot Tom crashes through the back door and practically blows it right off the hinges with one arm. I think, "Okay, seriously? Stinkweed stew, Bug Crunchers, and now a robot Tom, a killer 'bot?" He starts stomping toward me, and he doesn't look like he's coming over to ask me how my day is going, so I scramble though the gate and run with everything I've got down the gravel alley. I look back, and robot Tom is still coming. I can hear the sound of gears and electronics whirring as he walks almost as fast as I can run.

I'm totally out of breath as I hop fences and race through yards and alleys. I've lost him when I trip and fall hard, my shoulder slamming into the gravel in the alley. The potentium and my gun fly out of my hands and scatter. I grab the gun, but I can't find the gold metal ball. I'm scrambling around on my hands and knees, trying to find it when I see him come around the corner, moving fast. He's going to catch me. I get up and start running again, without the potentium.

Now I'm really scared, and my legs are almost dead. I can't outrun him … 'bots don't get tired. At least I don't think they do. I duck around a corner and dive into a bush up against an old brown wood fence and dig myself deep in the leaves with my back against the fence. I hear the steps coming closer.

Whirrr-chink, whirrr-chink.

I see his feet come into view right beside the bush I'm hiding in.

Whirrr-chink, whirrr-chink.

He stops right beside me, and I hold my breath. My hands are shaking as I grip my gun tight. I'm scared, but I think, *One step closer and metal-head is getting a BB sandwich.*

I can only see his feet, but I hear the whir of gears again. He must be looking around. I hear the sound of the camera eye again, and then he starts to walk off.

I sit in the bush, shaking, for about five minutes, until I can't hear him anymore. I crawl out, check to see that the coast is clear, and head for my house. Sam has to be there, and I don't suppose she likes being alone in this world with crazy robots all over the place, this twin world.

Twin World stinks.

I sneak back to Tiarra's house using alleys and side streets. I finally reach the front door and go in. I know exactly where to go. Sam and Tabatha, they're connected, I know it. We're all connected.

I go right to her closet and open the door and get tackled by my sister. That's twice today, but I don't care. We hug for a few seconds, and then she finally starts blasting questions at me, one after the other. I do my best to explain it all. I tell her about the dimensions, the Weed Eaters, the Meat Eaters, the Bug Crunchers, Tom, 'bot-Tom, Tabatha, and Tiarra.

Sam listens, and then she kind of looks at me funny and winds up with her right arm and punches me hard in the shoulder, and it really stings. Sam always could punch hard. She's just a little thing, small for her eight years, but she's wiry and quick. Her wavy brown ponytail hangs down over her baggy green T-shirt, the one that has "Skate Or Die" on the back. Her jeans are full of holes in the knees from skateboard tricks gone wrong. She's dressed tough, but tears run down her cheeks. Typical Sam—a contrast in opposites. One minute she's all cuddly and sweet, but back her into a corner and she'll fight and claw like a cat. The nurses at the hospital found that out the hard way when she was four years old and in the hospital with a high fever. She was calm as a clam until they tried to give her a needle. The next thing they knew, the fists were flying, and she was standing on the hospital bed yelling at the nurses to keep their hands off her.

"That's for getting me into this!" she shouts through her tears, and then she hugs me again. "Because I missed you, Sierra."

"Me, too," I answer, as I rub my sore arm. "That's why I came back … to get you."

We get up, and I start heading for the door. "We have to get to Tom, to tell him it worked, and about the 'bot."

"How do you know that he isn't the robot?" Sam asks.

"Because Tom wasn't a machine, and he wasn't trying to smash me before, that's why. It couldn't have been him."

"Okay," Sam says, "But if he even blinks once …"

"I know," I say, and we head for the door.

I'm surprised how well Sam is taking this. I thought she would be a basket case, but she's acting feisty, which is the Sam I know. That's a good sign. We walk down to the edge of the forest where the entrance to the cave is, and it takes me a while to find it. While we're walking, Sam is asking a million questions, and she seems more into the adventure than I was before. I guess now that we're together again, and she knows I have Tom helping me, she feels a lot better than she did when she was alone. I'm starting to feel better, too. It's even kind of exciting, in a way, and I have to admit, my sister's smart aleck attitude is actually a good thing, for once, because it reminds me of home.

We get to the giant stump entrance, and I load the BB gun and show it to my sister. "Just in case," I say.

I grab the hidden latch and open the door, and we climb in and shuffle down the tunnel.

"Your buddy can build a time machine, but he can't build a good fort?" Sam asks.

"Sam, it's a hideout ... did you expect a big shop on Main Street or something?"

We get to the end of the tunnel and slowly open the door. I see Tom standing at the desk, with his back to us. Just as he starts to turn I hear the sound of a camera click. Like the robot. There's nowhere for us to run this time, so I aim the gun to let him have it. The gun makes a snapping sound, and I hear the pellet smack him, and he yelps and dives behind some boxes behind the desk, crashing them over and scattering papers everywhere.

"Get ready to run!" I yell to Sam as I reload the gun. I turn and look, but Sam isn't going anywhere. She's found a piece of metal pipe about the size of a bat, and she's into batter stance and she looks like she's ready to knock robot Tom into left field.

Looks like we're here to fight.

"All right, metal brain, come and get it!" Sam yells as the dust settles around the boxes. She hasn't seen what robot Tom can do, but it's too late now.

Then it speaks.

"What the heck is going on? Don't shoot! Sierra, did you lose your marbles?"

It actually sounds a lot like Tom ...

"Show your face!" I yell. Tom slowly stands up with his arms in the air like it's a holdup. "Why did you shoot me? Are you crazy?"

His eyes both look normal, and it's clearly regular Tom. I lower my gun and signal Sam to ease up.

"Um, we thought you were a robot."

"You what? A what? Are you mental? You shot me in the butt!" Tom snaps, and he's rubbing his rear end with one hand.

Sam giggles and whispers to me, "Nice shot."

"Who is that?" Tom demands, looking at Sam.

"That's my sister."

"What? 'Kay, wait. You go back, bring your sister, so now there are three of us in this mess, and then for extra fun you came down here to shoot me in the butt?"

Sam giggles again. "Stop laughing," I tell her.

"Look, here's the deal." I explain, "When I got back home, Sam was gone, and her twin was in her place. So I came back here and got the real Sam, but first I stopped at your place, and there was a robot there, and it looked just like you ... and he tried to kill me. I only barely got away, okay? Then when we got here I heard the same camera noise he made, so I just thought ..."

Tom is pointing at the desk, right where his camera is sitting in the mess of papers.

"Oh," I say. "Uh, your camera sounded just like the robot's. Tom, listen, I'm sorry, and thank you for bringing me back. Your machine worked, it really did."

"It's okay" he says. "I would have done the same thing. Robot me, huh? Well that's random."

"It's never happened before, in all these years?" I ask.

"Nope. Something weird is going on." He begins to pace around, rubbing his chin. Then he hurries over to his papers and starts to shuffle them around. "Your sister being switched, too … something is happening. I knew it. My calculations show it would start to happen more, but I hoped it wouldn't."

"What is happening more? What do you mean?"

"Well," Tom starts, "in the last few generations, it seemed like the Bug-Crunchers were coming around a little more each year, and arriving in the same places, like they have worn their own jump path. At this rate they'll be everywhere in about ten years, plus maybe more and more people will get switched."

Sam pipes up, saying, "Speaking of munching, got anything to eat? I'm staaaaaarving."

"Over in the cupboard, there are some vegetables," Tom replies. Sam darts over to the food and starts scarfing down carrots.

"Listen," Tom says, "We have to jump again. I'm coming with you, and this time we're going forward in Twin World. We need more potentium, and we can't wait. I've done it before, but we'll go farther this time, to the future, about twenty years, because the potentium is more pure in the future, and we'll need lots of it, if there are more people in trouble."

"Wait," Sam says. "if you think you're going to leave me here alone in this cave with nothing but a BB gun and some salad, while a killer robot is stomping around out there, you can forget it. I'm coming."

"No way," I snap.

"No," says Tom. "We can't chance it. Sierra clearly is able to jump cleanly for some reason. It never works as well for me, and who knows what will happen to Sam. But she's right, we can't leave her here alone."

"Then I go alone," I say, and I walk over to the machine. "Fire it up."

"Just wait, I have to explain things to you." Tom says. Sam interrupts, not looking so tough just now. "Sierra, are you leaving again?"

I go over to Sam and put my hands on her shoulders. "I have to do this. I want to see Dad again. I want us *both* to. You need to stay here and help Tom. He will protect you. You can trust him."

"Okay, but get back here fast, so we can go home. Because the food here sucks."

"You have no idea ..." I say.

"Okay, Tom, what's the big plan?"

Tom pulls out some maps and starts drawing all over them, explaining to me how I'll go ahead about twenty years and how I have to get to the main factory for the Power-Wire Corporation, where I'll find good potentium. Tom gives me a backpack with some supplies. Then he shows me pictures he took on another jump. They are pictures of the fence around the factory and directions to the holes in the fence where I can sneak in. Tom explains how he had to do hundreds of jumps just to get a couple of pounds of potentium. He was able to go, but he always got bounced at the worst times, because he couldn't control it. Sometimes he would appear in the middle of a busy highway and almost get run over. With me, he can stay back, and it seems he can control things, because my last jump went pretty well, as far as I can tell.

"Only take the scraps from the pile on the north side of the factory yard. There's tons of it. Fill the pack, and we'll get you home. I'll give you two days. Forty eight hours. It's a modern city, and really crowded, so you should be able to blend in, but don't waste time. Don't draw attention to yourself: remember, it's the future, so you might stand out or look funny to people in your old-fashioned clothes."

"She always looks funny!" Sam jokes.

"Hey!" I say, but I smile at her. That's my sister, clearly her old self.

Besides, I'm kind of excited to see the future and all the modern buildings. I wonder if I'll see any cool flying cars and stuff.

"Ready?" Tom asks.

"Yup," I say, and go over and hug my sister. "You listen to Tom and stay safe. I'll be back before you know it."

I hear the machine fire up, and I see that Sam has her hands over her ears.

She loses her feisty attitude completely and latches on to me tight. "You better get back," she says into my shoulder and then lets go, and she looks pretty scared now. *What would Mom do?* I wonder. I remember a silly game Mom used to play in the car, where she would call out names to us like we were at NASA getting to launch a space ship. We'd answer "go flight" just like the guys in the movies, and she'd pretend to flip switches on the dashboard of our old Toyota before she drove away.

I turn to Sam, and I say in my most NASA-sounding voice: "Communications, do you read?"

Sam looks at me for a second, and then a smile grows on her face, and she answers "Go flight."

"Booster rockets?" I ask.

"We're go."

"Network?"

We're yelling now, as the noise continues to grow.

"We are go flight!"

"CAPCOM?"

"We are go for launch!" Sam shouts out, and I can barely hear her.

The ball bursts into view, and I step closer to it.

"I'll be back." I say, and I step inside.

Silence.

I'm lying on my side on the ground, and I can feel cold cement under me. I'm there. The future. I scramble to my feet, and I feel excitement build inside me.

The future.

I can't wait to see what it looks like. The modern cars, the cool buildings, the people. I want to get started, to get the potentium, to fix the mess. My eyes adjust to the light, and my head starts to clear. My legs are wobbly, but not just from the jump. They're wobbly from the sight I am seeing.

Total destruction.

There are no people, no buildings, no roads, no cars, no trees, no grass, nothing. Just piles of rubble, dust, and smoke. Everywhere, as far as I can see, it looks like a gigantic bomb was dropped here, wiping everything off the face of the earth. My hands shake as I pull out Tom's map, and I realize that nothing matches. There isn't anything to follow on the map, because all the buildings and roads are demolished. I realize in horror that I'll never find the factory in this mess, if it even exists at all anymore—and I am completely alone now.

In old Twin World, at least I had Tom and Sam, and even Tom's parents and other people. Compared to this, that was actually pretty good. I would trade this horrible place to be back there in a second. But now I may never get back. My heart jumps as I remember the potentium ball. Tom could get me back now!

But then I remember: I don't have it. I lost it in the alley when I was running from robot Tom. I forgot about that in the confusion before I left. I forgot to tell Tom. I drop to my knees and almost pass out.

I might be stuck here forever.

I just sit there on my knees, tears rolling down my cheeks, staring at the wasteland that used to be Earth. I have no plan, no potentium, no Sam, no Tom.

I don't know how long I sit there, crying, but it feels like hours, completely unable to do anything.

Until I hear the footstep right behind me.

Sam at the bat!

Chapter 10

Wasteland

I stop breathing and don't move a muscle.

I don't know what to do now. My mind races. A monster? Bug Crunchers? A dog? A bear? Suddenly I feel something cold and hard, like steel, closing around my neck from behind. I lunge forward and flip over to get away, but now I'm pinned to the ground. There's a steel hoop the size of my neck pushed into my throat, holding me on the ground, and it's attached to a rod that someone is pushing on, standing over me, holding me down.

"Keep fighting, and it's lights out, bug freak!" someone shouts.

The voice is that of a little boy. I have tears in my eyes from the pain of the bar on my neck, so I can't quite see who it is. It looks like a little kid, but it must be the strongest kid I ever met, and I can't get out. Finally I stop struggling, because I'm out of breath and having trouble getting air.

"Caaan't ... breathe," I say, gasping.

"Exactly. You want out, you better run when I let you go. I know you're alone, and I ain't afraid to use this bar to relocate your brain—your *brain*."

"Not ... Bug ... Cruncher," I say, barely able to speak.

The kid stops pushing and slowly lifts the bar off my neck and backs up, holding it with both hands like a sword in front of himself. I sit up and try to catch my breath, rubbing my throat.

"Why ... why did you attack me? Who are you?" I say, choking.

"You're not acting like a Bug Eater, just not a Bug Eater, huh?" he says.

I finally wipe my eyes and get a look at him. He's small and wiry like my sister. I bet he's only about seven or eight years old. He has curly brown hair, with an old set of ski goggles pushed up on his forehead, and he's filthy. His tan army pants are covered in dirt and stains, and his face is just as dirty. He's got no shirt on, and he's skinny, but I can see muscles in his arms as he points the iron bar at me. He clearly doesn't get much to eat, but he also looks like he could handle himself, even against an adult. The expression in his dark-brown eyes is changing from angry to puzzled.

"Where in the world did you come from, where in the world?" he demands, not letting the bar down.

"I came from the past, in a machine." I say, realizing as I say it that it must sound crazy. "The Bug Crunchers are messing up the world, and I came to try stop it."

"First of all ... as if!" the kid blurts out. "Try another story, another story! Second, too late saving the world, too late. It's done. Too late, mate, look around, look around, just around."

"Who are you?" I ask. "What year is it? Where are we?"

"What's with all the questions? What are you, a stalker? You dirty little stalker!"

This is one funny little kid.

"Okay, I'll play along," he says, finally letting his weapon down and leaning on it with one arm.

"Ben's my name, it's the year 2033, and we're in Aspen City, 20-33. Now how about you start telling me where you come from, history girl. Start telling!"

My heart sinks. Aspen City, my hometown, in twenty years. The future doesn't look very bright from here.

"Look, I wish I could prove to you where I'm from, but I can't," I say as I adjust my sitting position and pull off the backpack.

Ben sees the bag and jumps forward. "What's in the bag? Got any food? You got food? Big food? Got some? Got some?" Ben has completely forgotten his bar and is leaning in to try look into my bag.

"I dunno, I'll look." I say, telling the truth. Tom packed it, but I didn't really see what he put in. I open it up, and I'm rummaging around when I feel Ben's head right beside mine. He's practically sticking his head into the bag, looking for food.

"Whoa, easy, buddy!" I say, pushing him back. "You tried to choke me and now you want my lunch? I don't think so."

Ben steps back, looking kind of hurt. "Sorry, no lunch for days, I'm sooo hungry. No lunch. Just none today." He is standing there with his steel bar hanging down by his side, and he doesn't look tough anymore at all. He looks hungry.

"Please? Just please?" he asks.

"Okay, just relax, and I'll have a look."

I dig around, and at the bottom, I find a few chocolate bars and drink boxes. Thank goodness for Tom. This will help me win over this strange little kid because even though he tried to disconnect my head from my shoulders, maybe he's okay; maybe this world is the kind of place that teaches you to choke first and ask questions later.

I pull out an Oh Henry bar and hand it to him, and he attacks it. He runs and crouches down beside a big block of cement. He looks like some kind of monkey in a zoo. He bites off chunks without even taking off the wrapper, chewing and spitting out the wrapper pieces as he goes. I can see that more wrapper is disappearing than getting spit out, but he doesn't seem to care. When he's almost done, I hand him a drink box.

"The straw is on the side of the—" I start, but Ben has already torn the corner of the box off with his teeth and is sucking the juice down through the jagged hole. When the box is completely sucked flat, he rips it open and licks the juice left over in the corners. Then he stops suddenly, sits perfectly still, and cocks his head to one side, like a deer listening in the forest. He stays like that for at least ten seconds, and then he gets a really serious look on his face.

"We have to go. They'll be coming soon. It's getting late. They like late. They really do. I don't like late. I really don't."

With that, he starts half running, half sneaking, hunched over like he's playing hide and seek. Every once in a while he stands up and peeks over the rubble and then ducks down again.

I don't know who "they" are, but I can hear strange howling noises in the distance, and Ben suddenly looks really scared, and whatever he's scared of, I probably should be, too. Because the howling is getting closer.

Chapter 11

Gymnastics for ~~Girls~~ Boy

I follow Ben for at least twenty minutes.

We weave through a maze of junk and rubble as the sun, already red and partially blocked out by a gray haze, sets behind what's left of Aspen City. Finally he slows, then stops and turns and says "Step *exactly* where I step, unless you want to lose your head, your noggin."

He tiptoes in a zig zag fashion, with me behind him, stepping exactly in his footprints in the dust. I see he's got traps rigged everywhere somehow, which explains the zigzagging. We reach an opening in a half-destroyed cement building, and Ben looks over his shoulder, scans all around, and crawls into a small hole. I follow him inside, and he pushes a large wooden block over the hole behind me, and then lifts one end of a huge steel pipe down over the wood. We are barricaded inside. Then he pulls an old brown tarp over the wood and steel. "To keep the light secret, secret light."

I don't know what light he is talking about, because it's pitch black, and I can't even see six inches in front of my face. Suddenly there is a *bzzzzt* sound, and a flame appears. Ben is holding a small lantern. He has just lit the oil in the lantern by touching two cables from a car battery on the floor. The sparks from the cables lit the oil. Smart kid.

I look around at his little secret cave. It must have been some kind of basement storage room before the world got destroyed. It's only the size of a bathroom, or a really small bedroom, and Ben has a kind of nest in the far corner made of a pile of blankets. There are no windows, and the door to the right is completely blocked by a huge slab of cement that looks like it fell through the roof. Probably safer like that, I guess. There is a shelf with a couple of cans of food and bottles of camping fuel against the wall. He also has a lot of camping gear stacked in the corner: bows and arrows, cooking tins, camping stoves, knives, and camouflage hunting clothes. I notice that the arrows have the tips taped up with thick rings of duct tape, so that they aren't dangerous anymore. It seems strange that a kid who needs to survive in a wilderness like this would make his weapons less deadly.

"Better get some sleep, gotta hunt in the morning, show you the tricks, all the tricks," Ben says, and with that he throws me some blankets and curls up in his nest in the corner, but he doesn't close his eyes. He is staring at me as he lies there for a long time while I make my own makeshift bed with the blankets. He finally says to me before closing his eyes: "Good thing you came. I need to teach someone. She taught me, so I will teach you."

"Wait, teach what, who taught you? What do you mean?" I ask, but I already hear snoring across the room. I curl up under my blankets and drift off to sleep almost immediately, exhausted from everything that has happened since the day it all went weird at school.

I wake up to Ben shaking me and saying something. "Wake up, you, it's time to get food! Food, we need food again."

"What?" I mumble, still half-asleep. It seems like only a moment has passed since I closed my eyes, so it must have been a good sleep. I remember dreaming of my mom, my dad, and my sister, which I haven't done for years. It felt like we were all back together, like the old days.

"You! Get up, you!"

"Hey, I have a name," I say, still feeling sleepy.

"Well, tell me then. You didn't tell me then," Ben says.

It's odd how he repeats words like that. I suppose if you are all on your own your whole life, you might become a bit odd.

"My name is Sierra. How long have you been here?" I ask him.

He looks at me and smiles. "Sieraaaah. Sierr-rah! Sierr-raahhh." He's playing with it, sounding it out. Finally he says "Yep, I like it. I think I'll call you that."

"Uh, okay good," I say. "So, how long?"

"My whole life, obviously, my whole life," he answers, putting on a sweatshirt and tying his shoes.

"What's for breakfast?" I ask.

"Oh Henrys and juice!" Ben proclaims. "It was great! I'm full as a balloon! But you get rabbit. Oh Henrys are done. Just done."

"You ate all the food? Hey, that was all I had!"

"No" he says, "There's more, lots of rabbits, tons of rabbits. You can have those."

"I thought you had no food for days!" I snap at Ben.

"Some food, but just rabbits—I'm so tired of rabbits. Just tired."

"You little twerp!" I shout.

He pulls open the entrance barricade and hops out into the sunlight. I take a few moments to get my bearings and then climb out after him. It's not as sunny as I thought. It just looked that way from the dark hideout. The sky is still gray and dusty.

Ben is loading up a bow and arrow, but he's using one that still has a sharp end, and he signals me to follow him. We stalk around in the rubble for a bit, and finally we see it—a long-eared rabbit about fifty feet away. I feel awful that we have to kill it, but I'm really hungry. "Lucky day! Big day!" Ben whispers. Then he aims, and there's a thwack noise as the bunny goes down. "Sorry, bunny," he says quietly. "Just sorry."

Another one hops into view over 150 feet away, but Ben says "Holy, two! But too far, too far." I smile and say, "I got it." I pull out my gun and load. Soon we are roasting two bunnies back down in his fort.

"Gotta eat inside, don't want to attract them. Nice shot, Sieraaaah, nice shot."

"Who is 'them'?" I ask.

"Bug Eaters," he answers, chewing on a burned rabbit leg.

"Oh, Bug Crunchers," I say. "So it's true, they destroyed it all, huh?"

"Bug Crunchers?" Ben laughs. "Crunchers, munchers, spider lunchers. Good word, better than eaters. I'll take that one! Bug Crunchers, Bug Crunchers, Bug Crunchers!"

"So what exactly happened?" I ask.

Ben takes a big bite of rabbit leg and leans back into the wall. "I don't remember; I was so small, but Bee told me about it. Bug Crunchers started a war, and everyone joined in, until it was all gone, the whole world popped like popcorn."

"Who was Bee?" I ask.

"She was the other one from the light, like you, nice lady, just nice."

I'm stunned. There was another dimension jumper? How did she get back? Where is she? Who was she? "Wait, you saw the light?" I ask him.

"Yep. Yours was smaller, but hers was beautiful, just beautiful. She came, she taught me everything. Lots of words, how to survive."

"Did she stay long? Where is she? I have to know. It might be how I get back. Maybe she can help."

"No, she's been gone for years." Ben looks at the ground, and I can see tears welling up in his eyes. Then he straightens up and sticks out his chin. "She was here when I was little, for a couple of years, but I was little then, not a man, like now."

This poor kid has been surviving on his own all this time—he might as well be a man, because he would have had to grow up fast to survive.

"C'mon, Sierr-raahhhh. I have to teach you."

"Teach me what?"

"Gymnastics."

Okay, I think, *that's random.*

We're stuck in a future wasteland with Bug Crunchers out there somewhere and no food, but the boy wants to teach me gymnastics. I don't know what to think, so I decide to go along with it. "So, why gymnastics?" I have to ask.

"Because you can't outrun 'em: they're fast they are, just fast. You need to know how to get around like the place is a big playground, because they can't do gymnastics. You'll see. I'll show you."

The next day the lessons begin with Ben showing me basic rolls and swinging moves in the rubble. We train for months, eating small animals, canned vegetables, and talking at night. I want so badly to get out of here, but Ben insists. He keeps telling me that the time will come, but I have to learn gymnastics first, or I will be "Bug Cruncher lunch." Each day I get better, and the training helps time pass. Ben also takes me on tours of the rubble, miles from the fort. He tells me all about how he did these same tours. Sometimes we travel so far away that we have to stay overnight in other forts he has hidden in other parts of the city. We hunt by day and hide underground at night. I can see how living like this makes you tough. And I am getting stronger, too. My hands and feet and knees toughen up. I'm getting really good at gymnastics. We run through the rubble, flipping over blocks, swinging between poles, and rolling under obstacles. The only move I just can't seem to get is the big high-jump, and I've been getting more and more frustrated the last couple weeks. Ben can flip right over a six-foot-high wall like he was launched from a trampoline. After days of trying that one move, I'm completely demoralized, and I can't see the point anymore. I'm covered in bruises. I'm tired, and I lose my cool completely.

"I'm done with your stupid gymnastics," I say, and I start stomping back to the fort to make a new plan.

"Aw, Sierraaah, you are so close. You're almost ready to go over the Power-Wire wall."

I stop in my tracks. "Did you just say Power-Wire?"

"Yep, that's what we need—more yellow wire, Bee said. I was supposed to have it in my pocket, but I did not, it hurt in my sleep, so I did not."

"Wait, what? You know where it is? Why didn't you tell me? We need to go there right away!" I yell.

"No, you have to be able to vault the wall because it is too tall."

I can feel anger and hope brewing up inside me. "Listen, Bennnnnn, I'll vault the darn wall right now, right now, and then you are going to explain this and take me there, take me there, got it? Got it?"

Ben hops from one foot to the next with excitement. "Yes, yes, that's it! We'll go tomorrow, the weather is coming, once per year, will be here tomorrow, just tomorrow!"

I run back over to the starting point and gather all my strength, all my anger, all my sadness from missing my family, and I ball it up inside me like a bomb about to go off, and I start running. I spring hard off my feet, launch onto my hands, flip over just as I get to the wall, and plant my feet in the rubble at the base of the wall and spring off. I'm flying right over the wall, and I see it pass under me. I come crashing down on the other side and hit my back on a block, but I'm okay, and I stand up and am brushing myself off when I hear thunder crack in the distance.

"You did it, no doubt! Great vault, Sieraaaaah! Crappy landing, just crappy, but here comes the lightning, so tomorrow we get the wire!"

I'm feeling nervous and relieved as we walk back to the fort. Ben is positively buzzing with excitement, and he's going on and on about Bee and the yellow wire all the way back. He tells me how Bee said it was the key and that he should always keep it in his pocket, but how one night there was a big storm, and a huge flash in the fort, and Bee disappeared. He had always taken the wire out of his pocket at night, even though she told him not to, because it dug into his back when he slept with it in his pocket.

Ever since then he's been going to get more wire before the night of the annual storm, in the hopes he'd somehow end up where she is.

"Didn't Bee think that if you went with her it would just send your twin here?" I ask.

"No," Ben replies as we trudge through rubble. "She said that lightning strikes are powerful, awful powerful, and it was the future for her, so it would be like a Sunday drip."

"A Sunday what?" I ask, and then I realize what she said. Ben was so young then, he must have misunderstood her. I'm positive she meant a one-way trip. Maybe this means I can get back without messing up Tiarra.

We reach the fort and go in, and while I'm eating, he pulls out a worn-out old textbook and stares at the dusty cover. He gently wipes the dust off and comes over and proudly holds it out for me to take. "You earned the right to read this now," he says.

I take it as Ben goes back and sits down. The cover has the words "Gymnastics for Girls" in large red letters, but the word *Girls* is crossed out, and in its place is written *Boy*.

I laugh at that, and he points out that obviously he's not a girl, and obviously there's only one of him, so "Boy" was more accurate.

"It's my book, so I can write whatever I want on it, that's what Bee said. She taught me to read and write. See, I wrote my name in it. Above the note from Bee, Bee's note."

Ben flips to the first page and points out his name, and I just stare at it, totally confused.

Below it in messy kid printing is scrawled, "Ben Malkins."

"Ben … my name is Malkins, too." I'm having trouble absorbing this. Is Ben my brother, or my son in the future, a cousin? What are the chances? Is this just a fluke? "Don't you think that's odd?" I ask.

"Naaah," Ben says. "It's not my real name. Bee gave it to me. Said I should have a proper name."

I think, *That's odd, why would she choose Malkins?*

"Look," says Ben, "Bee wasn't even her name, either. I just called her that. She signed her real name after the first year she was here with me, right here. He points down below to the handwritten note.

"Merry Christmas, Ben, Love, Bethany."

I stare at the book, and I start crying, because I recognize the handwriting.

"Ben, this Bethany Malkins … Bee … that lady who was here with you … that was my mom."

Sierra vaults the wall

Chapter 12

The Wall

I cry for a long time.

I just sit there and rub my fingers on the words written by Mom, and I cry. She was here. She wasn't dead after all. She wrote these words right here. She touched this book. I squeeze the book and wish with everything I have that she were here now. All this time she was stuck in this other dimension, just like me, like Tom, like Sam. She must have somehow been sent to the wrong dimension, like us. She must have found Ben here when he was little and helped him survive, raised him like her own child while she tried to get back. She must have told him to have the potentium in his pocket so he could jump with her, but something went wrong and Ben didn't have the wire with him, and he got left behind. I think about how heartbroken she must have been ... or must still be, losing her family, and then Ben, who must have been like a son to her. It makes me want to scream. Where did she go, and why wasn't a twin sent to us in her place? Ben just sits and watches me, looking sad but not saying anything.

I'm sitting there crying when Ben finally speaks. "I understand. She was my mom, too."

"What? Your mom?" I sob.

"My new mom," he says. "I don't remember having a mom before her, so she said she'd be my mom. That's why I get the gold wire each year. I have to find her."

I find myself unable to think. It's all too much. I'm just clutching the book, crying, when Ben grabs me by the shoulders and looks right in my eyes.

"The weather is here, it's here. Just once per year. We have to get the wire tomorrow, or it's another year, another long year."

"But how?" I sob. "I don't know how it works! I don't know what to do!"

"I try something new every year," Ben says quietly. "Every year something new. She was building a machine. It blasted apart when she left, but we have to try to rebuild it. We have to try."

"But I don't know what to build, either, I just don't."

Ben cuts me off. "We'll figure it out, Sierra, figure it out, Sierra."

His words hit me like a bolt of lightning. *Figure it out, Sierra.* Just like Mom would say. And Dad would tell me to suck it up.

"Okay," I say, wiping my nose and rubbing the tears from my eyes. "Okay. We'll try."

"Hey hey, Sierrrraaa!" Ben shouts and jumps up. "I'll tell you the plan, and we'll go tomorrow! First I have to show you the machine. I built it, built it wrong, but maybe you can figure it out, Sieraaaaaah!"

We go outside, and Ben takes me around the side of the old building, where he shows me the exploded remains of a sort of tower made of steel scraps and wires. The other half of the building is completely collapsed, and the steel tower looks like a miniature drilling rig, mounted on the pile of rubble. Beside it are the skeletons of lots of other little machines he tried to build. There are lots of wires coming from the various machines, and all the wires are completely melted. "I remember she said the wire was the key, the key." Ben says, "But after the night she disappeared, there was no wire, just none." I look at his setup and try to follow the wires around. "Where do the wires go?" I ask.

"I run them to the fort, but it doesn't do anything, just nothing. Even when the lightning hits, nothing, just nothing ... except it straightens my hair sometimes, that's a kick!"

I look at the setup, and I'm sure that the electricity just grounds out in the cement. I understand electricity a little, from my dad. When I was in grade three, we built an electric machine for the talent show that made a pickle glow. I remember it only worked if I made sure that the whole thing made a complete loop. Otherwise the power didn't flow. The electricity had to have a wire to go into the pickle, but it also had to have another wire to follow back out, or it just stopped.

"Did you try making a circuit, a loop for the power to flow through?" I ask, and Ben just stares at me. Then he says, "Um, once I did connect both ends of a big wire, but then the whole wire just melted.

Too much power, I think to myself. "Okay, so first thing, we need to make the same circuit Mom did, then we have to find wire big enough for lightning."

I begin to dig around in the rubble to find a place where there is evidence of a circuit to the fort. I find a strange black line burned into the ground leading into the fort. I run around the front of the building and inside. Sure enough, there's a burned black ring along the wall all around the fort.

Ben is standing at the door watching me. "What did you find, find something?" he asks.

"Was this black line here the morning Mom went away?" I ask. "Yes, sir," he answers. "The wall sparkled for a second, and then the wire was gone, just gone."

"What color was the wire, Ben? This is important."

"It was gold. Gold for sure. But I don't remember how big, and the biggest wire I can find isn't gold, not gold at all."

I realize it was potentium wire. Mom had made a ring of potentium around the fort, in a loop from the tower. The lightning strike powered up the loop just enough to pull her out, and in the process it melted the remaining wire. But Ben hadn't kept the piece of wire in his pocket, so he wasn't connected. Mom couldn't have known what happened until it was too late, and the circuit was destroyed, so Ben was never able to get it going.

"Ben, I figured it out. We need wire, but not just for our pockets. We need lots. I can get us out of here."

Ben just stares at me for a second, and then he throws everything he has in his hands in the air, lets out a squealing whoop, and dives into the fort and starts ripping into his supplies. "We're going! Oh, we are, we are! Sierra knows! She's a Bee, she is the Bee, that's for sure! Need weapons, need shoes, need water, need pack, big pack, we're going, see ya, burned Aspen, oh, yeah, see ya, that's right, you suck, and we're outta here, me and little Bee!"

Ben continues to rummage and pack and ramble on excitedly to himself as I watch in amazement. Soon I begin to pack my own backpack with some basic supplies.

When Ben is done, he suddenly stops, sets his pack down, and flops on his nest. He looks around at everything thoughtfully, then he gets up and goes over to the shelf and pulls out a crayon drawing that he clearly drew when he was very young. It's a little stick boy with a stick woman smiling and eating a rabbit.

Ben rubs the drawing for a second and then stuffs it in his pack.

"We're really going, Sierra, aren't we, just going for real?"

"Yes, Ben, we are."

"I packed my picture of Bee for us, so when we meet her again, we'll recognize her, because ... I ... I sort of forget what she looks like."

"It's okay," I say. "Sometimes I forget, too. Get some sleep. We have a big day tomorrow."

I wake up to the blurry sight of Ben's face two inches from mine.

Startled, I pull back my head. "Wha?"

"Okay, here is the deal right now, just now. We go to the factory. One side only, the wall side. It was a fence, but they made a wall during the wars. The other side is the destroyed factory, and the Crunchers live in there, so we gotta be quick and quiet. The wire is just over the wall, but I didn't ever see long pieces. We might have trouble finding it. That's a fact."

I rub my eyes, and I see that there is an Oh Henry on my pack for me. "Hey, I thought you ...."

"I did," Ben confesses. "I took them, all three, but I kept one for myself, for later, just in case, just in case. But I couldn't do it; it's for you."

"Thanks, Ben." I say, and I eat it quickly. It tastes so awesome after months of burned rabbits. I give Ben the last bite, which he devours instantly.

"Okay, let's go." Ben says, and we head out.

As we're sneaking toward the Power-Wire factory, I notice that Ben has the arrows with the duct tape covering the tips, instead of the sharp ones he uses for hunting. "Why the dull tips?" I ask, touching one of the arrows.

"So they don't hurt them too bad," he answers and keeps sneaking along.

"Okay, run that by me again? What is the point, then? Don't you want to hurt them? They're trying to hurt us, ya know!" I say.

"No," Ben says, and he stops and looks out at the horizon, thinking for a second. "They were people once. Just people. They still are. They are messed up, good messed up, but just still people. They are mommies, daddies, kids. So my arrows knock them down but never kill, just never kill."

Then he begins sneaking along again, and I am left to think about the fact that this kid is smarter than the adults who destroyed the earth. No wonder Mom liked him so much.

After about an hour, we reach a hillside overlooking the factory. The factory is half-destroyed, with two old smoke stacks leaning over in opposite directions. There is a tall cement wall around a storage yard to the right of us, and on the left is the crumbled end of the building. I can see people walking around in the rubble on the left, and they're digging in the mess here and there. Every once in a while they start yelling and fighting. They look very unhappy.

"They don't really care about the factory, but that's where their base was in the wars, so they stay." Ben says. "C'mon, follow me."

Ben leads me down a hill through the trash, and he is tiptoeing now. We hear angry voices a few feet away. Ben grabs me and crouches down, and we sit holding our breath until the voices get farther away. We continue down around to the right until we're at the base of the wall. There's enough rubble to climb up and peek over the wall. I wonder why we needed to learn to vault, until I see that there's nothing on the other side to climb, just a sheer wall. Getting in will be easy, getting out … not so easy.

Ben signals me, and we both somersault over the wall and roll, each landing quietly on the other side on one knee. Good old Gymnastics for Girls and Boy. We sneak over to the pile of gold potentium wire and start quietly loading strips into our packs. I can't seem to find any long pieces. I look everywhere, and then I see it. Just inside the big, open back door of the factory is a perfect roll of it. I also see two Bug Crunchers right beside it, arguing. I point to it, and Ben shakes his head, but I whisper, "Yes."

I sneak over to the door and reach my arm in, just a few feet from the Crunchers. I can feel it. I have it in my grasp, and I pull, but it's caught on something. I pull harder, and it starts to come loose. I think, "Gotcha!" and then a whole pile of wire comes crashing down as I pull the wire free. The Bug Crunchers jump back from the falling wire, and then they see me.

"Ruuunnn!" Ben yells. I throw the wire over my shoulder and around my neck as I run for my life. I hear the Bug Crunchers running behind me and yelling "Stop right there! Stop! Get them!"

They're gaining on us as we get closer to the wall. You can do this, I think to myself, you did it before. But I realize I wasn't weighed down by all this wire last time! I feel a hand grabbing at my back just as I launch into my flips, plant my feet, and vault. I'm not high enough! My side hits the top of the wall, and I'm about to fall back inside when Ben's hand grabs my backpack, and he yanks me over the side. We crash down in the rubble on the other side in a cloud of dust. "C'mon!" Ben yells. "They'll come! They'll come!" We get up and keep running, and then we see them coming in from both sides of us. We put the gymnastics to work and vault over piles, swing over pipes, somersault over boulders, and roll under barricades. We keep going, past obstacle after obstacle, until my hands are blistered, and my knees are bleeding. Soon, their voices die away, and we aren't being chased anymore. We stop and look back, bent over, with our hands on our knees, panting.

"We did it, Sierra! Just we did, didn't we!"

"Yeah," I say. "I can't believe you do this every year!"

"I never take so much." Ben says, pointing at the roll I have over my shoulder. "They've never even seen me take it before."

We walk back the rest of the way and begin assembling the tower. We run the wire to the very top of the tower. We've created a huge potentium lightning rod that we hope will catch a lightning strike. There isn't enough wire to reach inside the fort, so we run the wire around in a loop at the base of the tower. We'll stand in there. It's our only chance. I'm having trouble finding a piece to hold the wire in place on the bottom of the loop, so I begin to search around in the rubble.

"I need to find some kind of a bracket." I tell Ben, and I walk back toward the path.

"Don't be far, Sierra, the weather is near, just near."

"Okay," I answer as I dig around about a hundred yards away. I find the perfect piece, and then I see the Bug Crunchers in the distance. Hundreds of them. Coming fast.

"Ben! They're coming!" I yell and I start running just as a bunch of huge lightning strikes start pounding all around us.

I'm running with everything I have. "The weapons! The gun! The arrows!" I'm yelling as I run. I look back and they're only about 500 yards away. Lightning is striking everywhere, and the wind is blasting dust in every direction. I reach Ben, and he throws me my gun, and we frantically attach the bracket to the tower. They're almost on us. One is getting close when Ben lifts his bow and clips the Cruncher in the forehead with a perfect dull-arrow shot. The Cruncher goes down with a thud. I see another one on my right and pick him off with my gun. He drops, and he's hurt, but not badly. *Just people,* I think to myself. We're standing at the base of the tower, side by side, facing the oncoming Crunchers.

Lightning is hitting everywhere, just yards away, and chunks of burned steel and cement are raining down on us. The sound is so loud I can feel it in my chest. Now the Crunchers are everywhere, and we're shooting back with everything we've got. I miss one, and he comes crashing at me, and Ben turns and whacks him on the head with his bow and knocks him out.

Then I remember something important.

"Wire in your pocket!" I yell to Ben as I take down Crunchers left and right.

"Yes!" he answers as he releases another arrow.

"Wire in your pocket!" Ben yells to me, and I stop and slap my hand on my jeans. It's there. "Yes!" I yell back.

The lightning and wind are so violent now, it's like we're being bombed by war planes. The Crunchers are all around us. We're running out of time. The lightening better hit our tower and get us out of here soon, or it's over for us. "Come on, stinkin' lightning!" I yell. *"Now!"*

I fire my last BB.

I look at Ben, and he's got one arrow left. There's a Cruncher coming right at us, and Ben nails him with his last arrow. Ben drops his bow, and I drop my gun. Ben grabs me around the waist and yells, "Thanks for coming, Sierra! Just thanks!"

I see another Cruncher lunge at us, and he grabs me, and I can still feel his hand claw at my shoulder as the air explodes around us with a deafening crackling noise and blinding white light.

Then everything goes black, and I hear screaming.

Chapter 13

Wanigas

The screaming wakes me.

I'm lying on the ground, on my side again, on cool grass. I open my eyes a bit, and it's not black anymore, but everything is blurry. Ben, is it Ben screaming? I try to open my eyes more, but they hurt, and the sunlight is too bright. I try to focus, and I can see Ben lying beside me, and he isn't moving, and he isn't screaming. I shake him, and he mumbles groggily. "We home, just home?"

I try to figure out who is screaming. I see someone running toward me. It's blurry, but I can see the person is being chased by a crowd of others. The screaming is getting louder. Suddenly they all stop, turn, and everyone starts running the other way. What is going on? The screaming dies. My focus gets better. Half of the running crowd is wearing one color, and the other—and then I see: it's a soccer game! The parents are screaming at their kids!

"Hey, why are you sleeping here?" I hear. "Get back from the sidelines, you'll get hit!"

I look up at the old man standing over u, wearing a hat that matches the colors of one of the teams.

"Go on, you punks, get out of here."

I get up slowly, and I grab Ben and help him up. We stumble off in search of something I recognize, to find out where we are, and more important, to find out when we are.

After wandering around as the sun sets, I start to recognize things.

Twin World. But when?

I find a newspaper box and look at the date on the cover page in the little window. 2013. We're back.

"It worked, Ben! It really worked!"

Ben is just gawking at everything. "It's so clean, just clean!" he says. "Can we get an Oh Henry?" he asks.

"Yeah, but first we gotta go see Tom and Sam."

We head for the hideout, and I lead Ben down to the entrance in the forest. It's a different season from when I left. Its autumn now, and the whole forest looks like it is on fire with all the red, orange, and yellow leaves. We open the hatch and head down the tunnel. I've been away so many months that I almost forgot what Sam looks like, and I'm so excited to see her again. I open the door, and I see Tom and Sam standing exactly where they were when I left. They turn and see me, and they both jump back and just about fall over.

"How did you get over there?" Sam shouts.

"It must not have worked," Tom says. "You only went across the room!"

"What?" I ask. I run over and hug Sam hard. "I missed you, Sam! Are you okay?"

"Missed me? Seriously?" Sam says. "You were only gone for a second! Get a grip, Sierra!"

"Who is that?" Tom asks, pointing at Ben.

"Ben's the name, came with little Bee, Sierra the little Bee, just Sierra, you see! Got any food? Good food? I could use the food!" Ben blurts out.

"So, Sierra ... you kidnapped Dr. Seuss?" Sam asks, eyeing Ben suspiciously.

Ben strides over to Sam and puts his face right up to hers, and she leans back like she's afraid he might bite her on the nose. Ben finally says, "You're pretty! I like your hair on your head. Shiny, just shiny!"

Sam looks at me nervously, not moving. "Uh, getting a little freaked out here ...."

"It's okay, Sam." I say. "He helped me get back. I've been trapped in the year 2032 for months. He was there his whole life, alone, so he's a little...different."

Ben leaves Sam and starts rummaging around for food.

"Months?" Tom exclaims. "Holy cow, you were only gone from here a second. Did you get some potentium wire?"

I take off my pack and drop it at his feet, and potentium wire spills out, lots of it. "Yeah. I got the wire. And it wasn't easy, let me tell you. The future is messed up."

"What?" Tom says, looking concerned. "What happened?"

Over the next hour I tell them about the destruction, the Crunchers, the tower, the gymnastics. Every once in a while Ben jumps in with his own version of things and puffs out his chest as he looks at Sam and tells how he saved me at the wall. Sam rolls her eyes but doesn't look like she minds the attention that much, either. Then I get to the part about Mom. Sam's jaw drops. Then she grabs me and hugs me, then jumps back. "Enough yapping already! We gotta fix this! Mom is alive, and Dad needs to know, and we need to find her!"

Sam is dead right, and I love that she's on board. "Yeah, Sam!" I say. "Tom, what's the plan?"

"I don't know yet. I just can't fit it together. I could send you back, but to do what? Where does your Mom fit? What happens to me and Ben? What is the key here? What are we missing?"

We hear Ben, over in the corner, repeating a word over and over. "Saginawwww. Saginaw! Saaa-ginawwwww."

"Ben. Really?" I ask. Tom and Sam are just staring at him like he has an extra eyeball in the center of his forehead.

"Why is he repeating my last name like that?" Tom asks.

"Your last name?" I ask, and then Tom points at the name on the notebook that Ben is holding.

"That's your last name?" Ben asks. "It's a good one. Yep, I think I'll call you that. Tom Saaginaaawwww. It's even fun backward. Wanigas. Wanigaaaasssss."

It hits Tom and me at the same time. We shout out in unison, "Principal Wanigas!"

A moment later we're out of the cave and headed for the school as the sun sets. I have the bag of potentium with me: I learned *that* lesson the hard way—never leave home without it. We have no idea how the principal is involved, or why his name is the exact reverse of Tom's, or how we could have missed that before. But one way or another, we need to do some investigating, undercover style.

We get to the school in the dark, and we sneak around back. "There's a utility door on the roof. I saw them open it once years ago when our soccer ball went up there in gym class," Tom says. "We have to find a way up there, because maybe the principal has records or something in his office. Maybe there's a clue in them."

We spot a fire escape ladder to the roof, but it's way too high to reach. "Ben, can you reach that and slide the extension down?" I say.

"Yep, oh easy, just easy."

"Are you kidding?" Sam exclaims.

"Just watch," I reply.

Ben jogs back about thirty feet, turns to face us, and starts running. He launches into a pair of flips and vaults up to the ladder, just barely latching on with two outstretched fingers. He climbs up like a monkey and slides the extension down, and we all climb up on the roof. Once we're up, Ben looks over proudly at Sam and winks. Sam rolls her eyes again and then says, "Okay, not bad."

We go to the utility door, and amazingly, it's not locked. We go inside and down some stairs and come out in the gym. We're about to go through the closed doors to the hall, when Tom stops. "Alarms," he says. We go around to the other side in the dark and find an open door. We sneak down the hall to the front of the school, and go into the office of Principal Wanigas.

"Wanigassss," Ben whispers.

"Okay, start looking in the file cabinets, his desk, anything. There must be something we can find," Tom says.

We dig through file after file, with no luck, until Sam finds a briefcase under the desk. She pulls out the large brown leather case, and sets it on the desk.

"This was hiding under the desk," she says. "Could be something."

I see a big black design on the top. It looks like a scary pair of eyes, almost like a tiger's or a panther's. It's stamped into the leather like a cattle brand. My mind has a fleeting idea that I've seen this before, but I can't place it.

Tom comes over and opens it. "I think this is something," he says.

There is a folder with the letters "W.A.S.P." on the cover. Underneath in smaller letters are the words: "Wormhole Advance Selection Program—Top Secret"

"What does that mean?" Sam asks. "I don't know yet," Tom replies.

Inside the folder are printouts of messages and diagrams. Tom pulls out one of the messages and begins to read it out loud.

"Dear Sergeant Wanigas:

The Insect Poison Serum is working well. Prepare for test transfer to Dimension Earth. The current wormhole connection is good, so we can begin building the base there soon. Please note that your twin, Tom Saginaw, is acting suspicious. The plan to keep him here is no longer effective. His robot copy is fully operational, and the eyes have been corrected to match human eyes, so Tom should be eliminated tomorrow."

"Tom! They're going to … eliminate you!" I say with a gasp.

"That's why my jumps don't work," Tom says. "He must be controlling them from here!"

"You got a robot twin! A 'bot twin!" Ben says, excitedly.

"It's not as fun as it sounds!" I snap.

"Just wait. There's more," Tom says and continues reading.

"Dimensions Alpha and Beta are online, and the new set of soldiers is ready for transfer. We are still unable to locate Professor Bethany Malkins. Her knowledge of our plan is still a problem. When she used the new machine to escape, she wiped out the codes, so we have no idea where she went. She must be found and eliminated. Until then, Dimension Earth transfer goes ahead as planned.

Sincerely, Commander Tsongas."

Sam puts her hand over her mouth and squeaks, "Mom …."

"We have to stop this, tomorrow," Tom says. "They're destroying worlds, and now they want to eliminate me and your mom. We have to get back to the hideout before they find us."

We leave the school and start walking back to the fort. Nobody speaks. Everyone is in shock about what we just found out. It's so much bigger than just being stuck here. It's about the earth being destroyed, people being eliminated. We don't know what that means, but we all think the worst.

Too many questions are swirling inside my head as we walk, and everyone else is just staring at the ground, except Tom. He mumbles and rubs his chin, all the way to the forest. I can't tell if he's thinking or losing his marbles. I also can't stop thinking that something is off; something wasn't right about the school. How could a top secret briefcase just be sitting unlocked under a school desk? I feel like my blood is turning ice-cold, and I shiver as an idea seeps into my mind: we are being set up for a trap. The feeling is shoved out of my mind when I think about Mom, about Dad, and about home.

Mom must have known about the plans and was trying to stop it. It has to be true. She was trying to save the world, and instead she got flung to another dimension through that machine. She must have been in a hurry, in real danger, and used full power. Maybe that's why her twin didn't come to us, and she went to the future: a one-way trip.

Finally, Tom speaks. "We need to get you back to Earth before they destroy it. We need to take out that robot. We need to get me home. Most important, we have to stop the principal. He seems to be some kind of leader, so if we can send him away somehow, it could buy us some time."

"Yeah," I say. "I get that, but we have to do all of those things when the sun comes up in a couple of hours, or it's lights out for Earth. We don't have enough time."

Tom stops and gets a funny look on his face. "What if we could transfer all of us, even the principal, the 'bot, everyone, in my machine, all at once? Then the principal couldn't control it because he'd be in the transfer himself. We would hope that the robot's brain would get fried by the high voltage, and we'd all go home."

"Okay," I say, as we start walking again, entering the forest. "It's an idea, but we'd have to find a way to get them down to your cave, all of us, all at the same time. It's the only place we know of where we control the jump. But it just might work, you know."

"But there's one more thing that is bothering me," I say. "Doesn't it seem strange to anyone else that it was so easy to get into the school, find the notes, and that they had the whole story laid out for us in there? Didn't it seem, I don't know, too easy?"

Suddenly Tom stops, and I see his jaw dropping. I look up ahead and see why. There is a giant, smoking hole where his cave and time machine used to be. There's nothing left, just a few burning trees around the hole, and the wreckage of Tom's destroyed machine everywhere.

We're too late, and any ideas that it was too easy are long gone.

Ben meets Sam

Chapter 14

Showdown

We all just stare at the gaping hole, and I feel numb.

Suddenly Sam breaks the silence. "Hey, you guys, wake up! We gotta hide! They might still be here!"

Sam has shaken us out of it, and we dive into the bushes nearby and hide. We sit quietly for a long time, watching the little remaining fires around the hole burn down until they are gone. Nothing seems to be happening here anymore, and time is slipping away.

"I think they're gone," Tom says, climbing out of the bushes and slumping on a log. "That machine was our only chance. Our plan doesn't work without it. What are we going to do now?"

I listen to the sadness in Tom's voice, and it unnerves me that he sounds so defeated. He has been through a lot, and he never gave up before. I think about how much I've been through, and Ben, too.

"Listen," I start, "I've been chased by a killer robot, traveled across dimensions five times, fought off a horde of Bug Crunchers, and built a time machine tower out of junk. We are *not* going to give up now. We can figure it out."

Ben jumps in, saying, "Yeah, Sieraaaaaah! Figure it out, just figure it out!"

"But we don't have a machine!" Tom shouts. "It's gone, don't you see?"

"What about the power coming in?" I ask, climbing around in the wreckage. "Can't we hook into that?"

"No, they would have cut it off. They're not stupid."

"Oh, I'd like to cut *them* off!" Sam grumbles, shaking her little fist. "Just one shot to the kisser, just one!"

Ben is grinning at Sam. "Yeah, yeah, one shot! I'm with you, Sammy, one shot, just one shot!"

Sam and Ben bump fists and cross their arms and stand there like a couple of gangsters.

I'm still going through it in my head, trying to figure it out. We built a machine from nothing before; there has to be a way. "Look, we just need another power source. Isn't there a power box or tower or something in town somewhere?"

Tom gets up and starts rubbing his chin. "Well, there is one place by the school, but it's right out in the open. Everyone will see us."

"But can't we just hook in at the last minute? Like get the wire all ready and then lure them in and *boom*, it's done," I say. "Because even if everyone sees, they won't know what's going on until it's too late."

Tom starts to pace around more quickly. This is what I wanted to see. This is good; he's thinking again.

"There is a green power box by the crosswalk," he starts. "If we took wrenches and removed the cover, there should be connectors in there. I watched one being installed when they were building the neighborhood about ten years ago. Thankfully, you still have the wire. But you'll have to be quick, and I'm not even sure which connectors to hook to."

"If we don't try it, nothing will matter." I say. "Besides, you can help me figure out the power box."

"No," Tom says.

"Why not?"

"Because we'll be getting Principal Wanigas and the robot. It'll be up to you."

"Okay, I'll figure it out," I answer.

Tom gets everyone to gather around, and he starts explaining and drawing out a plan in the dirt with a stick.

"Sierra, you go to my garage and get some tools, then head for the power box. Once you're there, remove the cover and set up a potentium ring around the box and out in a circle in the grass in front of it. Then take the two ends of the loop and pick out which two connectors you think are the right ones and connect one. Hold the other one and wait."

"What happens if I get the wrong connectors?"

"It'll straighten your hair!" Ben jokes. "It's a kick, just a kick!"

"Awesome," I say.

Tom continues. "I'll go to the principal's house. Ben, you go to the school. Let's hope the principal and the robot will be at one or both of those two places. Once we find them, we get them to chase us back to the box."

"What do I do?" Sam asks.

"You got a BB gun like your sister?"

"Well, I do at my garage, but I don't know if Tabatha does at hers," Sam replies.

"If there is one there, then you will be the firepower," Tom says.

"You go with Ben and stop at Tabatha's garage and see if she has one. Let's hope it will be wherever you keep yours. Then go with Ben to the school, but hang back a couple of hundred feet. The robot is fast, which is why Ben is going, but he may need you to use the gun to slow the robot down."

"Oh, I'll slow him down all right." Ben and Sam bump fists again. I roll my eyes, but I'm glad for it, too. The next few hours are going to take all the courage we've got, so if the kids are confident, we're way better off.

"Now listen," Tom says in a more serious tone. "It's got to be close. If we get too far ahead of them, they'll see us waiting at the box, and they'll know something is up. So we have to let them almost catch us, right until we're all standing inside the potentium circle."

"How will we get them holding some potentium?" Ben asks. "Because if they aren't, it won't work, just won't."

"Good point," Tom says. "I will try throwing some onto Principal Wanigas. Don't worry about the robot. He probably has some inside him, and even if he doesn't, we just want to fry his circuits anyway."

"How do we know it's the right amount of power or going the right direction?" I ask. "We need enough power to get you and Ben home without affecting your twins, but also low enough to switch me and Tiarra back."

"I think because we're not going back or forward in time, you guys will switch okay, and Ben is long since separated by so much time and space from his twin, let's hope it won't affect him, either."

"How do we know it will get us home?"

Tom pauses for a second and then answers. "We don't. I just don't know. I'm still learning about his, too. We'll have to take our chances."

I think about how risky this trip is going to be. All we'll really be doing is getting home—maybe. And even if we do, what happens to Ben? And the principal will still be planning to attack Earth, unless maybe, just maybe, trapping him there might delay his plans. Then I have a really spooky thought.

"Tom, I have a question."

"Yeah?" Tom says.

"You've been bouncing around in time for hundreds of years. So if we go back home for good, how old will you be?"

Tom looks at me with a stare that tells me he has thought of this, too. "I don't know. I could be ten again or 200 or dead. I really want to go home, though. I'll take my chances, just to see home once more."

After another short pause, he asks, "So, are we ready?"

He puts his hand out in front of him, and I put my hand on it. Ben slaps his hand on mine. Sam puts her hand on top.

"All right, guys," Tom says, "this is it. This is our last chance. Everything you've ever dreamed of in your future depends on this. Put all your anger, all your hope, all your homesickness, everything you got, into it. No matter what happens ... the future is up to us, to what we do in the next few hours."

We all just kind of stare at each other for a minute as the sun rises behind us through the trees.

Finally Sam gets an evil grin and says, "Dimension Earth, we are go flight!"

With that, we split up and head off to put Tom's plan into action.

I jog down alleys and side streets, sneaking like I'm back in the rubble of the future. I reach the garage behind Tom's house, but the door is locked. I'm going to have to break in. I grab a rock from the alley and smash the glass window in the door and reach inside to unlock the door. I see an old toolbox on the workbench and grab some wrenches and a hammer and stuff them in my backpack. Then I see it. An old Daisy Red Ryder BB gun. It's covered in dust and cobwebs, but I pick it up, and I hear the BBs rolling around inside. I take it with me, just in case.

I walk up the main street to the school, and I see the green power box by the crosswalk. Nobody in sight. I set my back pack down and pull out the tools. I try all the wrenches on one of the four bolts holding the service cover on, and to my relief, the last wrench fits. I try to remember what dad told me when we built a bike together last summer. "Lefty loosey, righty tighty," I whisper. I try to loosen the first bolt, but it's rusted tight. I get out the hammer and pound on the wrench a couple of times, and the bolt starts to move. I slowly turn the first bolt, straining with all my strength until the bolt is all the way out. My hands and arms hurt, but I start on the next one. Three bolts to go. I get the second one out the same way, and the next one comes out easily. One bolt to go. Just then I see a shadow over me. Someone is behind me. I turn around, and an old couple with a small dog is standing there.

"What are you doing?" the old man asks.

"Uh, I noticed this cover fell off, so I, uh, I'm putting it back on before someone gets hurt."

"Aren't you a bit young to be doing that? It's dangerous. Where are your parents?"

"Um, my dad just went inside to get something. He'll be right back out."

"Well, okay, but maybe stay back until he gets back."

"Okay, good idea." I say. I wait for a few minutes that seem like an hour for them to disappear around the corner. Finally I get to work on the last bolt. I can move the cover a little, but the last bolt is still holding it down tight.

That's when I hear Sam screaming.

"He's coming! Get ready!" she yells to me. I see Sam running at full speed, a BB gun in her hand, up the hill toward me, with the school behind her. Then I see Ben running with robot-Tom right on his heels. The robot reaches out and almost grabs Ben. Sam stops, drops to one knee, and takes aim with the BB gun, and I hear a crack. The robot falls face-first into the ground. But he gets back up and starts coming again.

"Not ready!" I yell, and Ben stops, looks back at the robot, and then darts off toward the playground. Sam follows them.

I go back to the bolt, and finally it moves a hair. I pound on it with the hammer, and it moves some more, and then the bolt spins loose, and the cover comes off.

I look back, and I see Ben swinging and flipping through the monkey bars, using the slides and bars and ladders as obstacles to keep distance between himself and the robot. The robot is struggling to keep up. Good old Gymnastics for Boy, I think.

Before I turn back to the power box, I see Tom running with everything he's got from the other side of the field, with the principal right behind him. He's going to be here in seconds.

Sam and Ben must see him, too, because they start running toward me, too. I throw the wrench down and dig the wire out of the bag. I look at the wiring in the box, and I see three switches to plug my two wires into: a red one, a green one, and a blue one. I have no idea which ones to pick, so I just jam one end of the wire into the slot below the red switch and start running wire around in a circle by the box. I'm holding the other end in one hand as I turn and see Ben and Sam running full speed right at me, and they are only a hundred yards away. Tom is also almost here, but the principal is gaining on him. It's going to be close. Suddenly I see the principal grab Tom by the back of the shirt and start to pull him back. I grab the old BB gun and aim. I have no idea whether this gun will even fire, but I pull the trigger anyway. To my horror, I miss, and I see a leaf in the trees behind them snap back. I missed high and to the left. Tom is struggling to get free, and his shirt is tearing. Sam and Ben are almost at me now. Okay, I think, down and to the right this time, last chance. I fire again. I hear a yelp, and the principal stumbles and lets go of Tom. He's trying to catch up to Tom again, but he's holding his forehead. Tom, Ben, and Sam are only a few feet away when I drop the gun and grab the other end of the wire. The three of them come crashing into the wire circle against the box, just before the robot and the principal come skidding up to us and step into the circle.

The principal is panting and sweating, and he has a big welt on his forehead. "You punks thought you'd get away, huh? Hey, what is that you have in your—" Before Wanigas can finish his sentence, Tom throws a loop of potentium over the principal's shoulders, and I jam the wire into the blue slot.

Sierra saves Tom!

Chapter 15

Dimension Earth

Once again, I'm lying on my side in a grass field.

Seems to me Tom's machines only know how to hit grass fields. I smell smoke from burning plastic. My hand aches, and I look down and see a big red scar on the palm. The burn is about the size of a golf ball, and it's already starting to blister. I must have gotten burned when I jammed the wire in the box. I turn my hand sideways and notice that the burn kind of has an odd shape, almost like tiger's eyes …

This thought is still floating around in my head when I roll over and bump against someone or something on the ground beside me. I'm looking right into an eye. The eye clicks like a camera, and I jump back in terror. But the robot doesn't move. I hear sizzling and popping, and I see smoke coming from its ear. The eyes go black and close for good.

I see Sam and Ben, but not Tom. I shake them, and they get up groggily.

"Are we home?" Sam says, getting up slowly. She jumps back when she sees the robot.

"It's okay. He's done," I say. I look around, and I see we're in the schoolyard. There are kids running everywhere, laughing and playing. A kid runs by and stops. "Hey, where did you guys come from?" he asks.

I recognize that kid. We're home.

"Hey, what's wrong with that guy?" The kid says, pointing at robot-Tom.

"Stay away from him," I reply. "He's grumpy."

"Weird!" the kid says, and runs off toward the playground.

Just then I hear groaning, and I turn and see Principal Wanigas getting up behind us. We all start to back away slowly when the principal grabs the collar of his jacket and speaks into it. "Mission aborted. Get me out of here. Now."

Suddenly there's a flash, and the principal and the robot disappear.

We all walk tiredly toward the school, and Sam hugs me as we walk. We did it. We're home, finally. I feel like crying, but I still can't find Tom. Where did he go? Is he trapped in yet another messed-up place?

A girl runs over and yells "Hey, Sam! Where have you been? We're playing tag!"

Sam gives me a big hug and takes off toward the monkey bars with the girl. We get to the playground, and Ben wanders off and stares at all the fun happening with a big grin on his face. "Just perfect, just perfect," he says.

I hear the voice of a teacher off to my right. "Mr. Saginaw! Mr. Saginaw! We've been looking all over for you!"

I turn and see a man that looks really familiar. He is smiling, and kids are running all around him.

He sees me and comes over and goes down on one knee in front of me. "Sierra. We did it."

I look at him closely. It's Tom. He's grown up. We hug for a couple of seconds, and then I see that he has tears in his eyes. He looks around and takes a big, deep breath. "It's good to be home ... thank you," he says.

"No, thank *you*." I say. "Did you just get here, too?"

Tom shakes his head. "Somehow I got here a week before you. I have a teaching job here now. I was really worried about you guys. Tiarra and her sister were here, and I helped them out, but they disappeared about twenty minutes ago when you guys showed up, so they should be home safe now."

Then Tom looks toward the parking lot and says, "There's someone here to see you."

I look over and I see my dad waiting at the edge of the schoolyard. He's just as I remember him, with his messy hair, three-day-old beard, jeans, and a T-shirt.

I see Sam running toward him. I sprint over, and we tackle him down and hug him hard.

"Hey, whoa!" Dad says, "It's like you haven't seen me for months!"

"You have no idea," I reply.

We all get up, and Dad says, "C'mon, let's go get some supper."

"Just wait," I say. I turn to look for Ben. I see him, with the school gymnastics team, which doing a workout in the field by the playground. Ben is right in the middle of a spectacular set of flips, ending with a double somersault and a perfect landing. The other boys and the coach slap him on the back and high-five him.

"Ben!" I yell. "Come get some supper!" Ben comes sprinting over to us, and he's grinning from ear to ear.

"Dad, this is Ben. He's going to be staying with us. I'll explain later."

Dad looks at Ben and says "Well, okay, if that's okay with his mom."

"Oh, I promise you it's okay with his mom." I say.

We're walking to Dad's truck when he says, "So guys, what should we have for supper tonight?"

I know exactly what we're having.

"Stinkweed stew and Oh Henrys," I say.

Home again!

Chapter 16

New Machine

Sam and I hike up through tall grass in the field behind the school.

It's springtime, and a warm, fresh wind is blowing through the field. I have a big sports bag over my shoulder. We stop, and I drop the bag on the ground. Sam unzips it and digs out two sets of ice hockey shoulder pads. We pull them over our heads and snap the waist straps into place. I reach in and pull out two black skateboard helmets. I see the headphones and microphone sets taped inside the helmets. We put on the helmets, and I flip a switch on the side. I hear Tom's voice in the earpiece. I think of Tom, back at the new base in the old abandoned shed behind town. I think of all the work we put into building the new machine over the winter. Months and months of work. A better machine.

It has to work. It just has to.

"Communications, do you read?" I hear Tom say in the earpiece.

I pull the microphone down in front of my mouth. "Loud and clear. Communications are go."

"Weapons ready?"

Sam and I pull our loaded BB guns out of the bag and slot them into place in the long holsters on our backs. "Weapons are go," Sam replies.

"Food supply?"

We take out three Oh Henrys and three juice boxes each and jam them into elastic loops on our shoulder armor. "Food supply is go."

"Powering up remote packs," Tom says. Through my earpiece I hear Tom flipping switches back at the base shack. Suddenly I hear a high-pitched whine rising from the battery pack taped to the back of our shoulder pads. I feel power surge through the cable running over my shoulder and into the fist-size handle strapped to my chest pad. Each of the handles has a big red button on top. I turn to Sam, and we pull our handles out of the straps and hold them out in front of us.

"Potentium packs are live," I say.

"Ready to save the future?" Tom asks, as the whine gets louder and louder.

"Roger that," I reply.

"Dimension Earth base, we are go for launch!" Sam yells over the loud whining noise.

Sam and I pull dark ski goggles down over our eyes, look at each other for a second, and then I say to Sam, "Let's go find Mom."

We all punch the red buttons at the same time. There's an exploding green ball of light around us, and we're gone.

Going back for mom

About the Author

Tim Brewster began this, his first novel, as a short story he shared with his children. He currently lives in Devon, Alberta, Canada.